J. H. Stevenson

Hell

and other poems

J. H. Stevenson

Hell
and other poems

ISBN/EAN: 9783337391003

Printed in Europe, USA, Canada, Australia, Japan

Cover: Foto ©Andreas Hilbeck / pixelio.de

More available books at **www.hansebooks.com**

HELL,

AND

OTHER POEMS.

BY

J. H. STEVENSON.

KANSAS CITY MO
RIGBY-RAMSEY PRINTING COMPANY.
1894

DEDICATION.

— —

INDEX.

TO THE READER.

To those who may this book review,
I wish to say a word or two;
Not that I care for what you say
About its merits either way.

But still most freely I confess,
It would be source of some distress,
To have it punctured through and through
As critics very often do.

But yet, perhaps, a savage thrust
Might be but nothing more than just;
For coat of mail, in all its parts,
May not resist the flying darts.

Whatever faults it may unfold,
I'm willing they should all be told;
That others may, to some degree,
Avoid mistakes unseen by me.

But yet some fellow, vain to show
How much, or little, he may know,
May seize the book to let folks see
He knows but little more than me.

Its grammar may be simply vile;
The language not in classic style;
But yet withal, some simple hearts
May find in it some touching parts.

TO THE READER.

Should you incline to be severe,
Just let me whisper in your ear:—
'Tis written in the Book divine,
That pearls are never cast to swine.

Don't stop at "Hell," that awful place
Prepared for those who fall from grace,
But pass along and you may find
Some things more pleasing to the mind.

But should this book one thought inspire,
Or raise the mind to something higher;
Or sweep one cobweb from the brain,
The work will not be all in vain.

However great its faults may be,
Don't let thy passion master thee;
But mount Pegasus like a man,
And write a better if you can.

Topeka, Kansas, May 15, 1894.

HELL.

Some people say there is a hell,
  Where wicked souls are doomed to go,
But this by others is denied,
  Who hold there is no hell below.
I've often heard the place described
  By certain preachers in my day,
And trembled like an aspen leaf
  As they its horrors did portray.

That such a place does not exist,
  I will not undertake to say,
Nor, from the knowledge I possess,
  Can I assert the other way.
That there's a hell, or that there's not,
  Is more than mortal man can know,
And in the soul's eternal flight,
  There's none can say where it shall go.

Were I to say there is a hell,
  Could I, with proof, support the plea?
Did I allege there's no such place,
  How could I prove it so to be ?
No matter what I choose to say,
  The myst'ry would remain the same,
But why should hell be made for man,
  Who knows not how nor whence he came?

If such a place has been prepared
  For erring mortals here below,
Can His chief attribute be love,
  Who, by His will, ordained it so?
'Tis said that man is born in sin,
  And all because one Adam fell,
And though his fall was pre-designed,
  His erring sons must go to hell.

When man was formed, the great I Am
  Approvingly the work surveyed;
And perfect from the Author's hand,
  In God's own image he was made;
But lest he perfect should remain,
  A tree was planted by on High,
With this injunction:—"Eat thereof,
  And on that day thou'lt surely die."

"Believe it not," the serpent said,
  "Partake thereof and thou shalt see
That it is good for man to eat
  The fruit that grows upon that tree."
Then Eve, as though not satisfied
  With all that in the garden grew,
By way of dessert had to go
  And eat the cursed apple too.

Then Adam, poor deluded fool,
  To make his ordained fall complete,
Advised by Eve, naught else would do,
  But he must take the fruit and eat.
And thus sin came into the world,
  And thereby death to all mankind,
And all because poor Adam did
  What God above had pre-designed.

When they had eaten of the fruit,
  Their eyes were opened where they stood
And for the first time then they knew
  That they were absolutely nude.
And thus it was they came to know,
  That male and female they were made,
But they, such knowledge to obtain,
  Divine command had disobeyed.

If by their eating of the fruit,
  Each other they could only know, ,
Then plain it is, that from the first,
  The great Creator willed it so.
Because when God created man,
  He said: "Be fruitful, multiply;"
Then told him not to eat the fruit,
  For if he did he'd surely die.

And thus was Adam left to choose,
  Between: "Be fruitful, multiply,"
And "Eat not of forbidden fruit,
  For if you do thou'lt surely die."
Was this not too severe a test
  That Adam had to undergo?
Because the fruit he had to eat
  If he his wife should ever know.

As though God could not bear the heat,
  So writers of the Bible say,
Before he ventured out to walk,
  He waited till the cool of day;
And as he walked in Eden's shades,
  Where Adam and his wife were placed.
They heard his voice and ran away,
  And hid themselves in greatest haste.

God called to Adam: "Where art thou?"
  And Adam answ'ring to him said,
"I heard thy voice and hid myself,
  For I was naked and afraid."
No fear expressed of punishment,
  For any wrong that he had done;
But when he heard the voice of God,
  'Twas being naked made him run.

"Who told thee that thou naked wast?
  Hast thou been eating of the tree,
'Gainst which thou wert by me enjoined,
  And whereof I commanded thee?"
Then making answer, Adam said,
  "It is the woman is to blame,
She ate the fruit, declared it good,
  And tempted me to do the same."

Said God to Eve: "What hast thou done?"
  And she, as simple as a child,
Answering said unto the Lord,
  "I by the serpent was beguiled."
Then next the serpent God addressed:
  "Because thou'st tempted Adam's wife,
Upon thy belly thou shalt go,
  And eat of dust thy length of life."

"Above all beasts and cattle too,
  Thou art accurs'd and still shalt be,
And 'tween the woman and thyself
  There shall be endless enmity."
And thus we learn from holy writ,
  How 'twas the serpent came to crawl,
But are not told how it did move
  Before the time of Adam's fall.

And from the text we must infer,
   That ere the time of Adam's fall,
Beasts must have undergone a curse,
   But now the serpent more than all;
For if on cattle of the field
   No curse upon them had been laid,
How could it be the serpent's curse,
   Than theirs still greater should be made?

God spake again to Eve and said,
   "For what thou'st done, this I will do,
Thy sorrow I will multiply,
   And likewise thy conception too;
In sorrow children thou shalt bear,
   And thy desire now shalt be
Unto the husband thou didst tempt,
   And he shall lord it over thee."

Next unto Adam spake the Lord,
   So Moses would have us believe,
And there on him he did pronounce
   The sentence that he should receive:
"Thou'st eaten of forbidden fruit,
   And here no longer shalt thou dwell,
And for thy disobedient act
   Thee from this garden I expel."

"And for thy sake curs'd is the ground,
   And henceforth be it understood,
That thorns and thistles it shall yield,
   And herbs shall be thy daily food;
And to the earth shalt thou return,
   From which thy body hast been ta'en,
For thou art nothing more than dust,
   To which thou shalt return again."

"From this delightful garden here,
　　Thee I will banish with thy wife;
I'll keep thee out with flaming sword,
　　Lest thou should'st eat the tree of life."
Then forth as wanderers they went
　　To seek some other place to dwell;
But in the sentence there pronounced,
　　God did not even mention hell.

Then Adam came to know his wife,
　　And she conceived and brought forth Cain;
In course of time was Abel born,
　　And by his brother he was slain;
All this in scripture is laid down,
　　And holy writ has made it known,
And preachers have declared since then,
　　We must accept it all or none.

And thus began the human race,
　　If Moses is to be believed;
But, writing at the time he did,
　　He might himself have been deceived;
For twenty centuries had passed,
　　Since Adam in the grave was laid,
When Moses undertook to tell
　　How all created things were made.

Thus far there's nothing heard of hell,
　　No mention made of such a place
As having been prepared by God,
　　For sinful men who fall from grace.
But priestcraft came, then hell was made,
　　A burning lake intensely hot,
Where endless torments waited those
　　Who would not worship as they taught.

Had Adam disregarded Eve,
  And let the fruit untouched remain,
Then sin to man would be unknown,
  And hell would wait for souls in vain.
But this, of course, would never do,
  The great Creator had a plan,
And long before the world was made
  Had foreordained the fall of man.

When man had lost this high estate,
  'Twas part of God's eternal scheme,
That he would send his only Son,
  Whose death the guilty should redeem.
What else could Adam do than eat
  The fruit of the forbidden tree?
Since such was foreordained by Him,
  Who was, and is, and is to be.

One thousand years, or nearly so,
  Did Adam on the earth reside,
And when his lengthened days were run,
  He peacefully lay down and died.
And thus from earth he passed away;
  His soul had winged its final flight;
Did it ascend to realms of bliss
  Or sink into eternal night?

Four thousand years from Adam's time,
  One virgin Mary did conceive,
And unto her a child was born,
  To save all those who would believe.
Thus to mankind a Savior came,
  Who died a ransom for us all;
But till He came, what had become
  Of all who died since Adam's fall?

What Savior died to ransom them?
  Whose blood cleansed them from guilty stain?
If goats and kids sufficed for them,
  Why should for us the Lamb be slain?
To them was given for a guide
  The law Divine and Prophets too;
If these were all sufficient then,
  Why not suffice for me and you?

But Christ was born, whose blood alone
  The lost and ruined can reclaim;
Yet millions of the human race
  Have never even heard his name.
When these from earth have passed away,
  Where shall their souls immortal dwell?
Because they never heard of Christ,
  Must they forever scorch in hell?

Ah, surely not, if God is love;
  No loving father would decree,
His child to be forever damned
  However erring it might be.
But why should those who know not Christ,
  When they have passed beyond the grave,
Escape the punishment of hell,
  If He, and He alone can save?

If from the first God had a Son,
  Who should to save mankind descend,
How he could be of woman born
  ' Is more than I can comprehend;
Yet preachers threaten us with hell,
  Unless we earnestly believe
That Mary, in her virgin state,
  Did God's begotten Son conceive.

God is the Father of us all,
   With Him there's no dividing line;
And Christian, Pagan, Heathen, Jew,
   All share his boundless love divine.
If He a Savior had prepared,
   Who should for sinful man atone,
Why should four thousand years pass by
   Before that Savior was made known?

And what is life? The spirit pow'r,
   By which our actions we control,
Which God imparted unto man,
   And made of him a living soul.
And what is death? The point at which
   The soul and body say farewell,
The one to mingle with the dust,
   And one to go where spirits dwell.

How oft sweet voices do we hear,
   Although the forms we cannot see;
They come like echoes from afar,
   Or whispers from eternity;
They come, but how we cannot tell,
   From whence we do not understand,
They softly glide across the soul
   Like rippling waters o'er the sand.

It may be dear, kind mother's voice,
   That speaks to us of deathless love;
It may be that of darling child
   With angel message from above.
Whence come these voices, which to hear,
   Makes heart and soul with joy expand,
Until our very thoughts are borne
   To blissfull realms of spirit-land?

Desponding soul, awake to joy!
　　Despair is not thy final doom,
Death's shadow's but a passing cloud,
　　And Hope illuminates the tomb.
Though preachers preach of endless hell,
　　Where unbelievers all are sent,
Kind, loving Nature cries aloud
　　Against eternal punishment.

Is there no heaven for righteous souls?
　　No hell for those who fall from grace?
When we are laid within the tomb
　　Where is the spirit's resting place?
Heaven is hope beyond the grave,
　　Which comforts mortals here below;
But that a burning hell exists,
　　Believing God, I answer NO.

If God is love, which I believe,
　　And if his love extends to all,
'Tis strange that Christ came not to earth,
　　About the time of Adam's fall;
For Adam then would had a chance,
　　And all his progeny as well,
To wash in the atoning blood,
　　Or die, uncleansed, and go to hell.

And blood-stained Cain, what hope for him?
　　Upon what Christ could he rely?
Before what cross could he kneel down,
　　And find the blood to purify?
Succeeding ages passed away,
　　And millions lived and also died,
And to eternal rest were borne,
　　For whom no Christ was crucified.

If racking pain, heartrending grief,
　The suff'rings mortals undergo;
If want and sorrow, sighs and tears,
　And untold wretchedness and woe;
If these are not sufficient hell,
　To satisfy a loving God,
Can he be merciful who would
　Still punish with severer rod?

But do the sinful of this world,
　Whose wicked hearts have Christ denied,
Sit side by side in paradise
　With those redeemed and purified?
Redeemed and purified by what?
　The blood of Christ shed on the tree?
But what of all the sons of God
　Who never heard of Calvary?

Think not the wicked shall escape
　Whom paths of vice and sin pursue;
For just as sure as God is God,
　They'll suffer for the wrong they do.
The soul in its eternal flight
　With kindred spirits shall abide;
Nor will the guilty seek to dwell,
　With those who have been purified.

We know the pious soul on earth,
　Will not with those associate,
Who take delight in wickedness,
　And with the sinful congregate;
Nor would the soul that's steeped in guilt
　Find any pleasure over There,
With those whose chief delight it is
　To worship God in song and prayer.

It surely, surely cannot be,
    When we are laid beneath the sod,
That spirit progress terminates,
    And fallen man is lost to God.
Why should the spirit not progress,
    When from the body it's set free?
What are a few short years on earth
    Compared to long eternity?

But preachers orthodox declare
    There is no hope beyond the grave,
And that the blood of Christ alone
    Is all that can the sinner save.
But surely there are other means
    . Laid down in the eternal plan,
By which salvation may be found
    To save poor, erring, sinful man.

To those who know not of the blood,
    Are they to have no means of grace?
Does not God's love, and mercy too,
    Extend to all the human race?
Are all to be debarred from hope,
    To whom no Christ was ever taught?
And where no cross was ever raised,
    Are faith and works to go for naught?

If nothing but the blood can save,
    Then hell is their eternal doom;
For preachers say there is no hope
    Beyond the darkness of the tomb.
Be not dismayed, poor wand'ring heart,
    The grave is not the final goal;
Beyond the dark and narrow cell
    There's hope for the immortal soul.

That Jesus suffered on the cross,
　By me has never been denied,
And many have, for conscience sake,
　Since then been worse than crucified.
What cruelties have been imposed
　By thumbscrew, torture, rack and rod,
By cruel fiends in pious garb,
　And all to please a loving God.

How many victims at the stake
　Have suffered in the ages past?
How many have upon the rack
　Been tortured till they breathed their last?
In dungeons many have been thrown
　To perish there for want of food,
Because they would not worship God,
　As mitred tyrants thought they should.

To not believe as bigots taught,
　Was deemed to be sufficient then,
To bring upon the victim's head
　The vengeance both of God and men.
Their deeds of fiendish cruelty
　Would make a savage blush for shame,
But all were done for dear Christ's sake,
　And to exalt his holy name.

They gloated o'er the blood they shed,
　And as by them each victim fell,
"Twas but another heretic
　Whose soul would find it's place in hell;
They clapped their hands in fiendish glee
　To see their helpless victims die,
And human holacosts they made,
　A loving God to glorify.

As though the Father of us all,
   Could any pleasure find or take,
In having children whom He loved
   Consumed by fire at the stake.
The being whom these tyrants served,
   Was surely not the God above,
For nature plainly makes it known
   That He is one of boundless love.

And those who did these fiendish acts,
   Good christians claimed to be, of course,
But if they were, in what respect
   Could fiends or devils have been worse?
The church they built must be upheld,
   It mattered not how many fell,
And for the unbelieving soul
   They even made a burning hell.

O, loving Christ! O, tender One!
   Who died and suffered on the tree,
What crimes have tyrants of the church,
   Been guilty of in name of Thee.
"Good will to men," and "peace on earth,"
   Were what Thou sought'st to inculcate;
But priestcraft came and introduced
   The doctrine of eternal hate.

That Christ excelled in purity
   All other men, is doubtless true;
The gospel that He always taught
   Was love to God and neighbor too;
But if He was Jehovah's Son,
   The offspring of the great Divine,
I'm at a loss to understand
   How He could be of David's line.

Theology so mixed has grown,
  And creeds have been so multiplied,
That mortals seeking after truth
  Become completely mystified.
Be not misled by doubtful creeds,
  But let thy acts be those of love;
Do what thy conscience says is right,
  And place thy trust in God above.

On Him we safely can rely,
  However far our footsteps stray;
His children He will not forsake,
  It matters not what preachers say.
Is it supposed a God of love,
  Will visit with eternal wrath,
The souls of those whose erring steps
  Have wandered from the narrow path?

What earthly father would condemn
  To suffer through eternity,
His erring offspring, whom he loves,
  However fallen they might be?
And can it be that God above,
  The source from which all mercies flow,
In His great love and tenderness,
  Will not still greater mercy show?

If God's chief attribute be love,
  Which I most verily believe,
How He can also hateful be
  Is something I cannot conceive.
Yet, if we take what preachers say,
  And do not walk the narrow path,
We're doomed through all eternity,
  To suffer his abiding wrath.

If Christ, by dying on the cross,
  Salvation purchased full and free,
Then it must be that all are saved,
  No matter what their faith may be.
But if He did not ransom all,
  There must be other means of grace,
Or hell will be the final doom
  Of nearly all the human race.

Are christian souls more dear to God,
  Than those of heathen or of Jew?
Is He the Father of us all,
  Or only of a very few?
Or does the great eternal scheme,
  By which salvation's to be wrought,
Include but those who have believed
  What priests and bigots may have taught?

Go forth and read from Nature's page,
  The character of God above,
And learn from vast immensity
  The boundless measure of His love.
See how He cares and doth provide
  For all the creatures here that dwell,
And can it be for man alone
  He hath reserved eternal hell?

Good thoughts in mind, good actions wrought,
  Kind words and deeds of charity,
A helping hand in time of need,
  'Tis these that God delights to see;
Nor will He question what our creed,
  Or at what shrine we knelt to pray,
Good deeds find favor in His sight,
  Be forms of worship what they may.

If I take Reason for my guide,
  And follow where it points the way,
Why God should have prepared a hell,
  Is really more than I can say.
For man, 'tis said, was perfect made,
  In God's own image formed was he;
He lives, he dies, his soul departs
  And goes into eternity.

The wicked soul will find its place,
  And join its kindred over there;
And brighter homes will be for those
  Refined and purified by prayer;
Ascending high and higher still,
  And still progressing as they go,
Until they join the perfect throng
  As pure and spotless as the snow.

But should I Reason cast aside,
  Like ship betossed I then should be,
With sail, and helm, and compass lost,
  Adrift upon the stormy sea.
Of this I'm sure, we nothing lose
  By doing all the good we can;
Nor will it make our chances worse
  To love and help our fellow-man.

What lies beyond the vale of death,
  Theology can not explain;
But this we know:—the seed that dies
  Springs forth to life and light again.
Man's thoughts may soar to lofty heights,
  But spirit-land he cannot see,
Nor can his gaze extend beyond
  The verge of vast eternity.

Be then content, vain, boastful man,
　　Great truths from you are yet concealed;
And what's beyond the mystic veil,
　　To spirits only is revealed.
Kind mother Nature gives to thee
　　A place upon her loving breast;
Thy spirit she will not forsake
　　When thou art laid away to rest.

Cheer up despairing, downcast soul,
　　A brighter dawn will break for thee;
And in delightful spirit-land,
　　Again loved faces you will see.
Behold sweet Nature's smiling face,
　　And all thy gloomy doubts expel;
Eternal Truth and Love proclaim:–
　　There is no everlasting hell.

PATERNAL ADMONITION.

You know, my son, I've always sought
　To teach you from your youth,
The principles of honesty,
　Integrity, and truth;
But fifty years experience
　Has changed your father's view,
For in the world as 'tis to-day,
　Such teaching will not do.

The truth of what I mean to say
　Some people may deny,
Who claim that men do not succeed
　Because they do not try;
They think that those in poverty
　Have but themselves to blame,
And that the fact of being poor
　Adds only to their shame.

I wish not to deceive you, lad,
　And frankly I confess,
That many are possessed of wealth
　Who once were penniless;
But yet, my son, while that is true,
　Just let me here remark,
That riches sometimes come to men
　By ways extremely dark.

The hawk, while soaring through the air,
   Swoops down upon its prey,
And there are hawks in human form,
   Less merciful than they,
And woe betide the hapless wretch
   On whom these hawks descend,
As well might lambkin ask the wolf
   Some mercy to extend.

O I have seen such sights, my boy,
   As brought tears to my eyes,
Have witnessed wives and little ones
   Turned out beneath the skies;
The little furniture they had
   Thrown out upon the way,
Because their monthly rent was due
   Which then they could not pay.

I've seen poor people's household goods
   'Neath chattle mortgage sold,
The stove not even left to them
   To save them from the cold;
The beds and bedding had to go,
   And all that they possessed,
The cradle where the baby slept
   Was taken with the rest.

I see I've touched a tender chord,
   But dry your tears, my son,
For what I have to say to you
   Is only just begun;
I've seen the shiv'ring children cry
   Around their mother's knee,
And wondered how a God of love
   Allowed such things to be,

No doubt as you grow older, lad,
　You'll come to understand,
That those who need conversion most
　Are not in heathen land;
The wildest savage ever roamed
　Would not the course pursue,
That brings to people such distress
　As self-styled Christians do.

But yet the heathen must be saved;
　The gospel must be spread,
While people in a christian land,
　May starve for want of bread;
And all because the golden calf,
　The god which they adore,
No matter how its maw is filled,
　Still cries aloud for more.

That I believe all men are bad,
　Must not be understood,
For take them as they are, my boy,
　The greater part is good;
But as you travel through the world,
　Strange characters you'll meet,
And you must always bear in mind,
　That tares grow with the wheat.

The mariner who sails the sea
　In search of foreign mart,
Avoids the dangers that he finds
　Marked down upon his chart,
And out upon life's stormy sea,
　Great hidden dangers lie,
Like treach'rous rocks beneath the waves,
　All covered from the eye.

There is a dang'rous rock, my boy,
  That frequently is met,
And many lives are wrecked thereon.
  It is the rock of Debt;
Avoid it by whatever means,
  For mark what you I tell,
The man in debt soon finds the place
  Described by some as hell.

Gay Pleasure's tempting shoals avoid;
  Beware of Siren's glance;
Be not allured by sparkling Wine,
  And shun all games of Chance.
Avoid the paths that lead to Sin;
  Let Vice detested be,
But greater curse than all of these
  Is that of Poverty.

You might, did others tell you this,
  Misgivings entertain;
But what I mean you'll understand
  As farther I explain.
Suppose a man is out of work,
  His children must be fed,
And daily they appeal to him
  To furnish them with bread.

He seeks for honest work to do,
  But vainly makes appeal,
Till he, to save his little ones,
  Must either beg or steal;
Want and hunger make him reckless,
  Death stares him in the face,
But still he shrinks from doing aught,
  Connected with disgrace.

Still lashed by cruel poverty,
　　He knows not what to do;
He suffers from its painful sting,
　　And pangs of hunger, too;
Night after night, with saddened heart,
　　His soul in anguish deep,
He sees the children whom he loves
　　Go supperless to sleep.

Soon follows dark despondency;
　　His heart begins to sink,
Despair now claims him for its prey
　　And drives him on to drink,
And narrow is the space, my son,
　　That Rum and Crime divide;
He next becomes a criminal,
　　And dies a suicide.

And now, my boy, perhaps you see
　　What poverty entails;
To peaceful homes it sorrow brings,
　　And fills the county jails;
It is the great prolific source
　　From which great vices flow,
The mother, too, of countless crimes
　　Entailing endless woe.

It may be said, in this great land,
　　Where ev'ry man is free,
And nature is so bountiful,
　　No man need idle be;
But yet, withal, the fact remains,
　　And cannot be ignored,
Some cannot get sufficient work
　　To even pay their board.

'Tis sad to think that this should be,
   But yet I must confess,
That men too often are to blame
   For much of their distress;
By boon companions whom they meet,
   They thoughtlessly are led,
And squander what they ought to save
   For years that are ahead.

Of course, the buoyancy of youth
   Must have some latitude,
But habits often they contract
   Which bode no future good;
'Tis not my wish to curb you, lad,
   But still you ought to know,
That wilful waste will surely bring
   Want, wretchedness and woe.

The depths and shoals of poverty,
   I've sounded o'er and o'er;
The sea of dire adversity
   I've sailed from shore to shore;
Yet I, in days now long since gone,
   Right royally did live,
When money through my fingers passed
   Like water through a sieve.

The art how to economize
   Was never taught to me,
Like young gazelle upon the plain,
   I roamed at liberty;
No bit or curb was on me placed
   To check my onward speed,
And on I ran without restraint,
   Like young unbroken steed.

But very soon I came to know,
　　For all my quickened pace,
I would, by those less fleet of foot,
　　Be distanced in the race.
The buffalo that leads the herd,
　　With hunters in pursuit,
Should he but fall, then those behind
　　Will tramp him under foot.

Thus, for a time, on life's great course,
　　I ran extremely well,
Until it happened in the race
　　I missed my foot and fell;
And while I in a helpless state
　　Lay prostrate on the ground,
Severely I was trampled on
　　And kicked for being down.

As oft as I would gain my feet
　　The struggle to renew,
The hounds again would be unleashed,
　　And after me pursue;
As tiger hunting down his prey,
　　So they kept on my path,
More fierce and unrelenting far,
　　Than lion in his wrath.

And all for what?   Because I owed
　　What then I could not pay,
And thus it was I was pursued
　　And hunted day by day;
And oft have I, with saddened heart,
　　In sorrow drooped my head,
As I have paid to creditors
　　What should have gone for bread.

I pray such troubles as I've borne
  May never fall on thee,
Although you had to bear your share
  Of those who fell on me;
If you can't pay for all you need,
  Then let the less be bought,
But always pay for what you get
  And pay it on the spot.

I know that kindness often prompts
  The rich to kindly deed,
And oft from tenderness of heart
  They help the poor in need;
But yet I trust that son of mine
  May never fall so low,
As be constrained to ask of them
  A favor to bestow.

If you your manhood would preserve,
  No favors of them ask;
Support yourself by honest toil,
  However hard the task;
Your independence still maintain,
  However poor you be,
For honest crust is sweeter far
  Than bread of charity.

Be not puffed up with self-conceit
  Should riches come to thee,
Nor think thyself of diff'rent clay
  From those who poorer be;
Be always civil in thy speech;
  Treat all with due respect;
Remember 'tis the empty head
  That stands the most erect.

If, by your own mismanagement
   Distress should fall on thee,
Don't undertake to shift the blame
   On those who prosp'rous be;
Don't let your mind be prejudiced
   'Gainst rich men as a whole,
For many are amongst them, lad,
   Possessed of noble soul.

But sharks there are amongst them too,
   Whose greed knows no control,
And who, to gain a little gold,
   Would sell their very soul;
They care for neither God nor man,
   Their hearts are made of stone,
And must have ten per cent. a month
   For money that they loan.

'Tis not the greatly rich, my son,
   That do the poor oppress,
And makes the crushed and stricken heart
   Shed tears of bitterness;
But O, the chattel mortgage fiends,
   Those hunters after spoil,
Their grip is worse than serpent's bite,
   Or Anaconda's coil.

Like beasts that roam the forest wide,
   In quest of daily prey,
These human wolves go prowling round,
   More merciless than they;
Their wounded victims bleeding lie,
   While o'er their forms they stand,
And, Shylock-like, with sharpened knife,
   Their pound of flesh demand.

I may be wrong in speaking thus
  To unsuspecting youth,
But it is nothing more than right
  That you should know the truth;
If wolves are prowling round the fold,
  The shepherd ought to know,
For then he might protect his flock
  Against the lurking foe.

These Shylocks hover round their prey,
  Like vultures round a corse,
They pick their victims to the bone,
  And never feel remorse;
And then on Sunday at the church,
  They're found upon their knees,
Endeavoring by mock appeals
  God's anger to appease.

Before the throne of grace they kneel,
  And ask that God will bless
The needy and the suff'ring poor,
  And others in distress;
Forgetful of the bleeding hearts
  To which they brought despair,
They think a God of love will hear
  Their vile, unhallowed prayer.

But churches now but temples are
  Where Fashion's vot'ries go,
To worship what? The living God!
  Alas, my boy, not so;
For soul that's pure and undefiled,
  If clothed in poor array,
Can scarcely find within their walls,
  A spot whereon to pray.

I don't decry the churches, lad,
  But this much I will say,
That some are far from being saints
  Who there kneel down to pray;
Their "Hallelujah" "Bless the Lord,"
  Will not for sin atone,
And prayer of ranting hypocrite
  Will never reach the throne.

But for the preacher's calling, lad,
  There must be due respect,
And if sometimes, for wordly things,
  Their Master they neglect,
That they are human bear in mind,
  And best of men may fall,
Nor should the preacher for his slips
  Be driven to the wall.

And preachers too, like other folk,
  Delight in well filled purse,
And if no better than the rest,
  'Tis certain they're no worse;
They have to live as others do,
  They have to dress and dine,
And money they must have, my boy,
  To buy religious wine.

But there are many preachers, lad,
  Who care more for their flocks
Than how to reap a rich reward
  From options, bonds and stocks;
They labor in their Master's field,
  With hearts both good and pure,
And carry smiles and cheering words
  To dwellings of the poor.

A lesson heretofore untaught,
  To you I would impart;
That I should have to teach it now
  Brings sadness to my heart;
And though I grieve to say it, boy,
  I here and now declare,
The standard by which men are gauged,
  Is money, ev'rywhere.

Let fortune raise, by sudden change,
  The beggar on the street,
And those who spurned him as they passed,
  Will worship at his feet.
Denude of wealth the millionaire,
  The favored of his class,
And those who doffed their hats to him
  Will spurn him as they pass.

All men can not be rich, my boy,
  But that's no reason why
The poor should be compelled to starve,
  Or beg, or steal, or die;
And my advice to you would be,
  Get all the wealth you can,
But never, to enrich yourself,
  Oppress your fellowman.

One thing to be remembered, boy,
  Insults you must endure,
And scoffs, and taunts, and insolence,
  So long as you are poor;
And knowing as I do, my son,
  What poverty will bring,
I'd rather see you in your grave
  Than subject to its sting.

The poor man's nothing but a clod
  Made from the coarsest clay,
And for his years of weary toil
  What has he for his pay?
A bite to eat, some clothes to wear,
  Make up his whole reward,
And even these are oft denied
  When times are rather hard.

Too bad, indeed it is, my son,
  Such lessons should be taught,
And you, without experience,
  May let them go for naught;
But mark you this, the tyrant's yoke
  I rather would endure,
Than suffer half the cruelties
  Inflicted on the poor.

No matter who the man may be
  With money at command,
He'll always meet, where'er he goes,
  With warm and welcome hand;
Among the guests at festal board,
  He'll have the honored seat,
But were he poor those self-same guests
  Would spurn him on the street.

Heed not at all what people say,
  For words are merely chaff,
A man with money in his purse
  At all the world may laugh;
But men with good and honest hearts,
  As pure as dew at morn,
Will have to bear, if they are poor,
  Scoffs, insolence, and scorn.

I cannot tell you half, my son,
　　Of what I've had to bear,
The days of mental agony,
　　And nights of dark despair;
The insults, taunts, and jeers I've borne,
　　And how my heart has bled,
As all in vain I begged for work
　　To earn my children bread.

Of troubles that afflict the poor,
　　I've had a goodly share,
And oft have I, from cruel want,
　　Been driven to dispair;
The pangs of hunger I have felt,
　　And oft with tearful eye,
Have I implored the living God
　　To kindly let me die.

E'en now, my son, it starts a tear
　　To think what I have borne,
And how I suffered from the stings
　　Of supercilious scorn;
But though severely I was scourged
　　By man's inhuman rod,
I never parted with my trust
　　Or lost my faith in God.

As out upon the desert wide.
　　Green spots are sometimes found,
Which make the weary pilgrim's heart
　　With hope and joy abound,
So may be found on life's great plain,
　　At intervals apart,
Sweet streams of pure benevolence
　　That flow from tender heart.

It may not here be out of place,
  To let you understand,
That money is the magic pow'r
  That rules in ev'ry land;
And as society exists,
  Poverty is a curse,
And men have got no right to live,
  Who have an empty purse.

'Tis money moves the world, my son;
  'Tis money makes you friends;
And when the purse is empty, lad,
  The best of friendship ends;
O'er men of ev'ry class and clime,
  It holds despotic sway;
The beggar and the potentate
  Its mandates must obey.

E'en preachers for the golden calf
  Their Master have denied,
And lessons taught by Holy Writ
  From them have cast aside;
They grasp for wealth with miser's greed,
  And still for more they crave,
Preferring treasures of the world
  To those beyond the grave.

And now, my son, to principle
  Give not too willing ear;
And when the voice of conscience speaks,
  Be not too quick to hear;
But should'st thou mingle with the flock,
  Be meekest in the fold,
And don't forget whilst praising God,
  The one that's made of gold.

Remember this, the world is not
    What it may seem to you,
For I have always kept, my son,
    The bright side to your view;
But had the picture been reversed,
    You need not now be told,
The god that people worship most
    Is one that's made of gold.

The world is full of sham, my boy,
    And gross hypocrisy,
And men are not, as you suppose,
    What they appear to be.
For those who look the most like saints
    Are deepest dyed in sin;
And those who seem the most devout
    Are hypocrites within.

I do not like to say it, boy,
    But for your sake I must;
The world is filled with such deceit,
    One knows not whom to trust;
And he in whom your faith is placed,
    And count your dearest friend,
Like fleeing rat from sinking ship,
    Deserts you in the end.

Some time ago I had a friend,
    Whom trouble brought to grief,
And cheerfully with all I had
    I came to his relief;
But fortune's wheel has turned since then,
    He's up and I am down;
No more he gives a friendly hand,
    But meets me with a frown.

I would not have you steel your heart
    'Gainst doing kindly deed;
Nor would I have you stint your hand,
    At helping those in need;
And should some poor unfortunate,
    To you his wants address,
Give cheerfully of what you have
    To aid him in distress.

The greatest rogues that live, my boy,
    Assume high moral airs;
And lips of mock religionists,
    Pour out the longest prayers;
And when some earnest trusting soul,
    Petitions to the Throne,
These pious frauds, from wicked hearts,
    Send forth responsive groan.

I don't profess to be a saint,
    And I confess, my son,
That there are things I now recall
    I would I had not done;
But hypocrite I never played
    My neighbor to defraud,
And never thought that cheating men
    Was dealing fair with God.

Against the sanctimonious rogue
    Be ever on your guard;
But yet I would not counsel you
    Religion to discard;
The church is not to blame, my boy,
    If members fly the track,
Nor is the flock to be condemned
    Because a few are black.

As men are measured in the world
    By systems now in vogue,
'Tis money makes the gentleman,
    The want of it the rogue;
It places on the coward's brow
    The laurels of the brave,
And makes of man a demi-god,
    The want of it a slave.

It dresses vice in silken robes,
    And elevates the knave,
And many of its darkest crimes
    It hides within the grave;
It crowns the vilest renegades,
    Makes right the foulest torts,
From churches makes religion fly,
    And justice flee from courts.

This final admonition, lad,
    Impress well on thy mind,
Don't ever undertake to be
    More honest than mankind;
In dealing with your fellowmen,
    Act just as others do,
And while you do not swindle them,
    Let them not swindle you.

My counsel now is at end,
    And some things I have told.
That would have been to me, my son,
    More pleasing to withhold;
And though the picture may, as drawn,
    Seem rather strange to you,
The strangest part of all is this:
    That ev'ry word is true.

THE FATAL APPLE.

Had Adam at the first but known,
   And let forbidden fruit alone;
Or had he, 'neath the apple tree,
   But said to Eve, "Go, tempt not me;"
Or but remarked, "The apple's small,
   My dear, I pray you, eat it all;"
How happy now we all should be,
   From ev'ry vice and trouble free.
But when his wife declared it good,
   He ate the apple where he stood;
What next they did may not be known,
   As he and Eve were there alone.

But some contend 'tis by the fall
   The human race exists at all;
And had he not the apple ate,
   Eve would have lived in virgin state;
But, for my life, I cannot see
   How such a thing as that could be.
For they were ordered by on High,
   To "fruitful" be, and "multiply,"
And that the law should be obeyed,
   Both male and female they were made;
And had the apple never grew,
     Nature would teach them what to do.

Just why he ate we cannot tell;
　　Enough to know he ate and fell,
And what before had been concealed,
　　To him was there and then revealed,
And from the seed of knowledge sown,
　　A tree of unbelief has grown.
Men now no longer condescend
　　The head to bow, or knee to bend,
Before a God they cannot see,
　　Who sits enthroned in mystery;
And thus in self-conceit and pride,
　　The living God they cast aside.

In olden time folk used to meet
　　Devoutly at the mercy seat,
And old and young assembled there,
　　Most fervently would kneel in prayer;
Nor did they care how they were dressed,
　　They went to worship and be blessed.
So in the darkened days of yore,
　　Folk safely slept with open door;
But in this wise, enlightened age,
　　Bolts, locks and bars are all the rage;
And rogues from knowledge but derive
　　The greater skill on which to thrive.

Knowledge has spread to such degree,
　　That nothing but a fool is he,
Who bows before the great Unknown,
　　Or kneels to pray before His throne.
The worshipers of olden time
　　Who entered church with thoughts sublime,
And knelt before the throne of grace,
　　Would now be sadly out of place.

One God they had and knew no more,
  But there are gods now by the score,
Style, Fashion, Wealth, Ambition, Pride,
  And many other gods beside.

The altar of the Good and Just
  In ruin lies amidst the dust,
And other gods usurp the place
  Where once was set the throne of grace.
The preacher, too, for worldly dross,
  Discards the teachings of the cross;
And sermons are prepared to-day
  To suit the ears of those who pay;
For members might his fee curtail,
  Did he their vanities assail;
For preachers, just like all the rest,
  Now practice that which pays the best.

They preach God's vengeance, to be sure,
  But that is only to the poor;
While those who swell the yearly fee,
  Find grace and mercy full and free.
Ye hypocrites, is God above
  Not one of mercy, truth and love?
Would ye from those his love withhold,
  Who cannot purchase it with gold?
Is this what knowledge teaches you,
  To damn the crowd and save the few?
Go preach such stuff at Fashion's throne,
  But leave the poor man's God alone.

Church usefulness has been destroyed,
  By knowledge wrongfully employed;
And sects have risen by the score,
  Condemning what they praised before.

All in bitter strife contending,
    Some assailing, some defending,
Each spitting forth envenomed spleen,
    Forgetful of the Nazarene;
And thus in hate they drift apart
    As far as God is from their heart;
Each lays Jehovah on the shelf,
    And makes a god to suit itself.

Believing that their faith is right,
    Each sect goes forth to spread the light,
And preach to men, what they conceive.
    The doctrine that they should believe;
And soon the branch begins to be
    A rival to the parent tree.
Creeds have become so multiplied,
    And truth has been so mystified,
That now 'tis more than man can do,
    To tell what's false and what is true,
And thus like ship with rudder lost,
    On waves of doubt he's roughly tossed.

What aid can knowledge render man
    To solve the great eternal plan?
So vast the sea he would explore,
    He gets no farther than the shore;
And when at last his work is done,
    He's just about where he begun.
As beast or fiend that tastes of gore,
    Will smack his lips and thirst for more,
So he whom knowledge once acquires,
    Becomes inflamed with new desires;
And thus, forever, men are led
    By something always just ahead.

The humble peasant, all untaught,
    Finds peace within his little cot;
Though coarse the fare on which he dine,
    He eats it with contented mind;
In God he has abiding trust,
    And in contentment eats his crust.
Let knowledge enter at his door,
    His peaceful days are then no more;
His mind by doubts becomes betossed,
    His former faith in God is lost,
Away he sails on boundless sea,
    And drifts to infidelity.

And what is gained for man to know
    The secrets of the depths below?
Or why the planets stretched in space,
    Move round the sun at such a pace?
The universe is so arranged,
    That Nature's law can not be changed.
Astronomers may space explore,
    And planets find not found before;
May tell when comet's drawing near,
    And just the time 'twill disappear,
But Science nor Philosophy
    Can comprehend Infinity.

Man may the course of planets trace,
    But can't explore unbounded space,
And countless worlds, yet unrevealed,
    In realms of space may be concealed,
And knowledge only serves to show
    How little finite mind can know.
Though wisdom great man may attain,
    He can not with it all explain

The mystery that lies concealed
  In smallest flower of the field;
Or how it ever came to pass,
  The growth of simple blade of grass.

Man's knowledge, after all, is naught,
  Compared with that that's still untaught;
And though more wisdom he might know,
  Than Solomon of long ago,
With him he'd say, when all was done,
  "There's nothing new beneath the sun."
Though man the lightning may command,
  He cannot even understand
The flow'rs that bloom so sweet and fair,
  And give such fragrance to the air;
The cause that makes their colors blend,
  Is something he can't comprehend.

Take man himself, and who can claim,
  To know from whence or how he came?
Or who can undertake to say,
  How long on earth he has to stay?
Or tell what flight the soul may take,
  When it the body doth forsake?
Can man, with all his knowledge, say
  Why eyes are black and others grey?
Why *this* man's short and *that* one tall?
  Why one is large, another small?
However high his thoughts may soar,
  He knows he *is* and knows no more.

Then why a phantom still pursue,
  Since 'neath the sun there's nothing new?
You stretch your hand to pluck the peach,
  But better see beyond your reach;

And if the better you might get,
  You'd see beyond still better yet.
As some green spot on desert plain,
  The weary pilgrim seeks to gain,
But ere 'tis reached, with staff in hand,
  He sinks and dies upon the sand;
So men by knowledge are led on
  To seek for something still beyond.

By light of knowledge, it is said,
  The world much better hath been made;
That men to-day are gods to see,
  Compared with what they used to be,
And children now more wisdom know,
  Than sages in the long ago.
Suppose all this to be the case,
  What better is the human race?
Are people not as scarce of dimes,
  As those who lived in olden times?
Does poverty not still exist,
  And do not paupers swell the list?

Do not avarice, lust and pride,
  Still in the human heart abide?
Does neighbor love his neighbor more,
  Than neighbors loved in days of yore?
Is not the bliss of wedded life,
  Destroyed by jealousy and strife?
Do nations not still go to war,
  To slaughter, plunder, maim, and scar?
Does Vice not vaunt her shameless face,
  Where Virtue could not find a place?
Are murder, theft, and other crimes,
  Less rampant than in olden times?

The spread of knowledge has, no doubt,
   Great changes wrought and brought about;
For instance: In the days of old,
   The robber said, "Hand out your gold;"
But greatest robber now is he
   Who robes himself in sanctity.
He walks the streets with pious air,
   At church he makes the longest prayer,
In Sunday school he plays a part
   To hide his bad and wicked heart;
But wash away the thin veneer,
   A full fledged robber will appear.

The truly blessed of all mankind,
   Are those of unenlightened mind,
Who, looking forth on earth and sky,
   Find knowledge that will satisfy,
And though untutored, bend the knee
   And bow before Infinity;
Whose minds by dogmas are not ruled,
   Whose hearts in simple faith are schooled,
Whose thoughts forever upward soar
   To Him whose works they still adore,
And read in all they see abroad
   The everlasting love of God,

Numerous gods do men create,
   Vindictive gods, and gods of hate;
Relentless gods to love unknown,
   And some make gods of love alone,
But let their gods be what they may,
   As is the model so are they.
The god that christians have designed,
   Is one of love and hate combined;

For those who are within the fold,
  There's endless peace and joy untold;
But those outside the narrow gate,
  Are doomed to everlasting hate.

The man on search of knowledge bent,
  Becomes a prey to discontent;
He's ever reaching, but in vain,
  For something that he cannot gain;
He longs for things to him denied,
  And dies at last unsatisfied.
But happy he with no more light
  Than guides his heart and thoughts aright.
For, though with little knowledge blest,
  His mind enjoys sweet, tranquil rest:
His day's work done, he takes his ease,
  With happy children round his knees.

The African, ere captive ta'en,
  Enjoys the freedom of the plain;
The savage, roaming wild and free,
  No king more happy is than he;
He roams at large without restraint,
  Adorned with breech-cloth and with paint.
He does not care a single straw
  About the niceties of law.
Nor is his mind disturbed to know,
  How planets in their orbits go:
In Nature's book enough he finds
  To satisfy untutored minds.

Knowledge destroys in its advance,
  The bliss enjoyed by ignorance,
The mind is ever working out
  Some problem still involved in doubt,

And this no sooner is made plain,
　　Than others follow in its train,
And these, if solved, but yield their place
　　To others coming on apace,
And thus an active, cultured mind,
　　A moment's rest can never find,
But constantly is tossed and rolled,
　　Like some great ocean uncontrolled.

The christian goes to heathen lands,
　　With sword and Bible in his hands,
And there he finds contented race,
　　But all without the means of grace;
So many souls must not be lost,
　　They must be saved at any cost.
The christian then with zeal begins
　　To turn the heathen from his sins,
And points him to the narrow way
　　That leads to everlasting day;
The heathen then can choose between
　　The sword, and blood of Nazarene.

Before the christian did assert
　　His right the heathen to convert,
They dwelt in peace, and only sought
　　To worship as they had been taught,
And why are they for this to blame,
　　Since christians only do the same?
Faith of each denomination
　　Is but the growth of education;
And those who christians claim to be,
　　In creeds most widely disagree;
And children take the parents' view,
　　Whether the doctrine's false or true.

It matters not where christians go,
    The seeds of strife they always sow;
They carry into foreign lands
    Discordant creeds and firebrands;
The heathen must be gospel crammed,
    Or be forever lost and damned.
Has God, who rules the world above,
    Debarred the heathen from his love?
And will he not incline his ear,
    The heathen's earnest prayer to hear?
The form of worship plays no part,
    Where purity dwells in the heart.

Why undertake to christianize
    The heathens under foreign skies?
Why undertake to change their faith,
    For which they'd gladly suffer death?
God hears the prayers of all who plead,
    And knows not either sect or creed.
If heathen souls they seek to save
    From being lost beyond the grave,
Why go so far to save so few,
    And leave uncared for millions, who,
In christian lands, are lost to grace
    As much as all the heathen race?

What better are the heathens here,
    Than those who dwell in other sphere?
Or are they so completely lost,
    Their saving is not worth the cost?
Are not their souls as dear to God
    As heathen souls that dwell abroad?
Then why don't preachers in their zeal,
    To serve the God to whom they kneel,

A little more attention pay
   To heathens not so far away?
Or do they think that heathens here,
   Don't come within their sacred sphere?

If what the scriptures say be true,
   The preachers now are very few,
Too few, alas, and far between
   Who imitate the Nazarene;
He preached the gospel free and wide,
   By sea-shore and on mountain side.
But preachers now are far too wise,
   To trust the Lord for their supplies,
For well they know they'd poorly fare,
   If all their faith was placed in prayer;
The days of miracles are o'er,
   And show'rs of manna fall no more.

'Tis very well for them to pray,
   "Our daily bread give us this day,"
For with a good, round yearly fee,
   Their prayers will surely answered be;
Not only bread will be supplied,
   But many other things beside.
Not all the preachers, be it said,
   Are thus supplied with daily bread,
For there are those we sometimes meet,
   Who scarcely get enough to eat.
And not because they do not pray,
   But that their prayers don't bring the pay.

And there are those who have, forsooth,
   Been crammed with learning from their youth,
So greatly crammed with moods and tense,
   No room was left for common sense,

And all the knowledge they possess,
 But adds the more to their distress.
What doth their learning signify,
 If they can not their wants supply?
Instead of blessing it's a curse,
 And renders their condition worse;
Much better they had learned a trade,
 Or gone to work with pick and spade.

Men have been known, and not a few,
 Well versed in Greek and Latin too,
Could works in French translate with ease,
 And quote correctly Socrates,
Who had, by hunger's stern demands,
 To earn their bread with blistered hands.
Then be content with common schools,
 And stop producing college fools;
Let foreign tongues aside be laid,
 And teach instead some useful trade,
For skilful hands will yield more fruits,
 Than all the Greek and Latin roots.

What cares the swarthy son of toil
 At what degree the pot may boil?
What cares the man who swings the flail
 About the length of comet's tail?
Or what cares he who tills the ground
 How planets in their course go round?
But let the pastor have his pay,
 He cares not how the flock may stray,
And men of high and low degree,
 Love money more than Deity,
For people, as in days of old,
 Still worship images of gold.

To golden calf they may not bow;
  They may not kneel to golden cow;
They may not worship at the shrine
  Of golden beast of any kind,
But in their hearts, though unrevealed,
  A golden image is concealed.
Better to be untutored clod,
  Respecting man and fearing God,
Than be an educated drone
  Without a cent to call your own
Trusting to what is in your head
  To furnish you with daily bread.

But parents now who have the cash,
  Must stuff their sons with college trash,
And then, when once they graduate,
  They think they're born for something great,
But soon they find, they'd better fared,
  If they to work had been prepared.
Some men are happy as can be,
  Who scarcely know their A B C;
They toil and labor all day long,
  And lighten work with joyous song;
Their day's work done they homeward start,
  With mind at ease, and merry heart.

Bright, happy children run to meet,
  Their father coming up the street;
A loving wife, with smiling face,
  His coming greets with fond embrace,
And all untutored though he be,
  No potentate more blessed than he.
I'd rather son of mine should learn,
  By honest toil his bread to earn,

Or have him taught some useful trade,
  By which his living might be made,
Than have him stuffed and crammed at schoo'.
  To be an educated fool.

A MIDNIGHT VISITATION.

As from the distant belfry tow'r,
  The bell proclaimed the midnight hour,
I ceased to read.   "So late" I said,
  "How very fast the time hath fled."
I turned the leaf the place to keep,
  Then went to bed and courted sleep;
And very soon the line was crossed,
  Where wakefulness in sleep is lost.

But scarcely had I closed my eyes,
  When, very much to my surprise,
I heard a noise that startled me,
  And wondered much what it could be.
It was not knock upon my door;
  It was not footstep on the floor;
It was not sound of beating rain,
  Or tapping on the window pane.

Believing there was meant no harm,
  I did not feel the least alarm;
But yet the noise so sudden came,
  I woke surprised to hear the same.
It came with such a whirring sound.
  As made by birds, when from the ground
They mount on wing, and take to flight,
  When dog or huntsman comes in sight.

I lay and thought how to explain
  The noise I heard; but all in vain,
And, wond'ring, to myself I said,
  "By what could such strange noise be made?"
For what it meant, or did portend,
  I really could not comprehend,
And as I lay bewildered quite,
  There came a voice:—"Get up and write."

The words I clearly understood,
  But being not in writing mood,
I answered back:—"Why this request?
  The hour is late, I want to rest."
I turned myself upon the bed,
  Adjusted pillow to my head,·
And sleep was stealing o'er me when,
  "Get up and write," I heard again.

Again I found myself awake,
  And said aloud:—"For mercy sake.
Must I this phantom voice obey?
  Or have my senses passed away?
Am I bewitched? Has reason fled?
  Am I entranced here in my bed?
Am I to have no sleep to-night?
  Then came the voice:—"Get up and write."

I rose in discontented mood,
  And almost swore as there I stood:
I struck a match and lit the light,
  And then I asked what I should write.
Again the voice came plain and clear:
  "Sit down and write what thou shalt hear,
Nor think it strange there comes to thee,
  A voice from out eternity."

I realized a sense of awe,
  I heard the voice; no form I saw;
Again I asked: "What can it be,
  Has taken such a hold on me?"
I'll shake this phantom from my brain,
  And try to go to sleep again:
But strive to shake it as I might,
  The voice kept urging me to write.

Then since escape I could not find,
  I to the task myself resigned,
Concluding that some great control,
  Had ta'en possession of my soul.
Just what it was I can't explain,
  But as resistance was in vain,
I took my pen, the ink drew near,
  And what I wrote will follow here:

"O, man, if thou would'st understand,
  What doth pertain to spirit land,
Seek wisdom from the source on high,
  And learn to see with spirit eye:
'Tis not for mortal to behold.
  The things that spirit life unfold;
As well might he whose void of sight,
  Attempt to grasp a ray of light.

Man gropes in darkness like the blind,
  In search of that he cannot find;
He lifts his eyes, but fails to see
  What lies within eternity.
No mortal eye can penetrate
  The boundless realms of spirit state;
Yet spirits often come, I know,
  To visit those on earth below.

To men, no doubt, this may seem strange,
  But when to spirit life they change,
Such wondrous things will then appear,
  As mortals never dream of here.
Man breathes but cannot see the air,
  Yet it surrounds him ev'rywhere;
Invisible to mortal eye
  The wind speeds on and rushes by.

Don't think it strange that I should say
  Man cannot spirit land survey;
On sun resplendent in the sky,
  He cannot look with steady eye.
Then how can he expect to dwell
  On what ten thousand suns excel?
To gaze on splendor thus combined,
  The light itself would strike him blind.

'Tis not for man to look upon
  What lies within the great Beyond;
Yet from that bright and higher sphere,
  Oft spirits come to mortals here.
They feel their pow'r, their voice obey,
  But how they come they cannot say,
They realize a presence near,
  Although the form may not appear.

Is it more strange that this should be,
　Than things already known to thee?
Then wonder not when thou art told,
　That things exist you can't behold.
Canst thou immortal thought command,
　Or touch it with thy carnal hand?
Or canst thou, with thy mortal eye,
　Behold its form in passing by?

Since then thou canst not comprehend
　How thoughts are formed, or how ascend,
Think it not strange that spirits bright,
　Can not be seen by mortal sigh..
But yet conditions may arise,
　And mortals so etherialize,
That spirit forms may come to view,
　And talk with them as I to you.

In vain to think thine eye can trace
　The spirit's form through boundless space;
Or that thy narrow, finite mind
　All truth can grasp, all knowledge find;
For couldst thou comprehend the whole,
　Thou'dst find that thine immortal soul,
Compared with vast immensity,
　Is less than drop is to the sea.

Could man his sphere of thought extend,
　And greater truths still comprehend;
Or could he stand upon the shore,
　And secrets of the deep explore;
Or stand upon the sea-girt coast,
　And number all the starry host;
Or count the sunbeams one by one,
　His wisdom would be just begun.

So great is unbelief in man,
  Concerning things of spirit land,
They will not give attentive ear
  The truth of spirit life to hear.
They grovel on in darkness still,
  Submissive to their stubborn will;
But here's a truth, in nature found,
  Seed will not spring from barren ground.

Man must not think to change the course
  Of Nature's law, or psychic force;
Or that a spirit pure within
  Will seek companionship with sin.
Be not deceived, if unprepared
  No spirit message will be heard;
If uncongenial it would be,
  No spirit form will come to thee.

There is no dross in gold refined:
  Pure thoughts spring not from carnal mind;
From fountains pure, clear streams descend,
  But vice and virtue do not blend.
In spirit life, as it is here,
  Each spirit seeks congenial sphere;
And when they come to visit earth,
  They come to those of spirit birth.

And even now, unseen by thee,
  A lovely spirit form I see,
And by its side a youth appears,
  If told by time, scarce twenty years.
Other spirit forms they meet,
  Whom they embrace and fondly greet:
Whatever message they impart,
  Receive it with believing heart."

I dropped the pen when this was said,
  And from the table raised my head,
And, looking 'round, I saw quite clear
  The spirit form of mother dear.
" Mother," I cried, and from my seat
  I rose the spirit form to greet;
I knew her well, though from my birth
  I'd never seen her face on earth.

I prayed aloud:—"O, Spirit Pow'r,
  I thank Thee for this blessed hour.
I thank Thee I have lived to see
  The form of one so dear to me;
I thank Thee for the spirit sight,
  I thank Thee for the spirit light,
I thank Thee I can understand
  The voice that comes from spirit land."

I saw the smile upon her face;
  Her ev'ry feature I could trace;
The joy that filled me as I knelt
  Was such as mortal never felt.
Enfolding me in fond embrace,
  I clearly saw her darling face;
And when she spoke, so sweet her voice,
  It made my heart and soul rejoice.

"I come, my son, with words of cheer,
  To tell you I am always near,
And have been with thee in the past,
  And will be with thee to the last.
I know thou'st suffered much, my son,
  And great the dangers thou hast run;
But greater still hast thou been spared,
  Because my spirit voice you heard."

Whilst telling me of mother love,
   And speaking still of things above,
"I must," said she, "this truth declare,
   All are not happy over There.
What's known as death don't end the strife
   For higher, purer, better life;
And soul that's purified below,
   To higher spirit realms will go."

As with delight her voice I heard,
   More brilliant still the light appeared;
And close by mother, standing there,
   I saw a youth extremely fair.
Some pow'r within impelled me on—
   "Is this," I asked, "my brother John?"
And then I heard dear mother say,
   "Before you came he passed away."

"He was my first-born, you the last,
   And when from earth my spirit passed,
He came and took me by the hand,
   And welcomed me to Summerland.
My son, my son, didst thou but know,
   How I have watched o'er thee below;
I've followed thee on land and sea,
   And ever have been close to thee."

"When thou wert wand'ring all alone,
   In foreign lands and all unknown,
Thy wand'ring footsteps still to guide
   Was mother ever by thy side.
When dangers great did press thee hard,
   Thy mother's form was there to guard;
Though mortals may this truth deny,
   True mother-love can never die."

"Though in your world there's grief and care,
    And pain and sorrow ev'rywhere;
And minds betossed, and tearful eyes,
    And breasts that heave with mournful sighs;
Though souls are pierced with painful darts,
    And anguish deep rends many hearts;
How much the sadness would increase,
    If mother spirit-love should cease."

"Though clouds may rise and dim thy sky;
    Though sorrow comes and loved ones die;
Though burdened down with grief and care,
    Be not a prey to dark despair.
Remember this:—Where'er you be
    Thy mother will be close to thee;
And those who spirit life deny,
    Shall realize it by and by."

"Doubt not, my son, whate'er you do,
    That spirit life is real and true;
Were it not so, would I be here,
    To give you words of hope and cheer?
Farewell, my son, but ere I go,
    A mother's kiss I will bestow;"
A zephyr seemed to fan my cheek,
    I felt the touch, but could not speak.

THE TRIUMPH OF TRUTH.

For ages the world had lain under a cloud,
   And Reason had slumbered in darkness of night,
While Truth had been sleeping wrapped up in a shroud,
   And Darkness obstructed the coming of Light.
Mankind had been groping their way like the blind,
   And those who would guide them but led them astray,
But Light found a pathway to enter the mind,
   And all the dark clouds are now passing away.

Great cobwebs had gathered and clouded the brain,
   And mildew and mold hung so thick on its wall,
That Truth, ever striving, but striving in vain,
   Could not find a loophole to enter at all.
But Light now is spreading all over the earth,
   And Mind, disenthralled, soon unfettered shall be,
While Truth shall illumine and gladden each hearth,
   And Conscience, enfranchised, declare itself free.

The clouds are dispersing all over the sky,
   And Truth's shining banner once more is unfurled;
From ocean to ocean goes forward the cry,
   That Falsehood and Error must flee from the world.
The chains have been broken, the fetters are gone,
   And men hail with gladness the coming of light;
Triumphantly Reason now sits on the throne,
   And Truth has emerged from the darkness of night.

If conscience and reason were given for naught,
   And we must still follow where bigots have trod;
If we must accept all the nonsense that's taught,
   Then tell us, we pray thee, the purpose of God.
Tell us for what was our reason imparted,
   Ye teachers of dogmas of orthodox schools;
If ye have the pow'r to curb it and thwart it,
   'Twere better had God made the rest of us fools.

Though preachers may lash us from pillar to post,
   And threaten us all with the heretic's doom;
And tell us that we are eternally lost
   And hell is our portion when laid in the tomb;
While such kind of preaching may have its effect,
   To frighten poor souls still benighted and blind,
A l sensible people can not but reject
   A doctrine so hateful to God and mankind.

God gave us Reason our minds to enlighten,
   And Truth He implanted our footsteps to guide;
Love is the light that our pathway should brighten,
   An l Hope is the anchor at which we should ride.
Priests, by their teaching, turned Reason to blindness,
   And Truth they supplanted by falsehood and prayer;
Love they converted to hate and unkindness,
   And Hope they enshrouded in gloom and despair.

A God that was loving for them would not do,
   His work that was perfect they thought to excel;
A god they set up of most horrible hue,
   And made for poor mortals a bottomless hell.
All kinds of torture by them were projected,
   That devils could think of or demons devise;
Blocks they constructed and scaffolds erected,
   And innocent blood rose in flames to the skies.

To kneel to their monster if any declined,
   The thumbscrew and rack stood conveniently by;
And those who rejected what they had designed,
   Should perish from earth and as heretics die.
Lovers of truth stood appalled and affrighted.
   While dark Superstition its banner unfurled;
Kingcraft and priestcraft together united,
   And light for a season passed out of the world.

So vengeful in wrath was their vindictive god,
   That mercy to mortals could never be shown;
So hateful in person, so cruel his rod,   [throne.
   That Truth veiled her face and relinquished the
Victims were slaughtered by scores and by hundreds,
   The octogenarian and golden-haired youth;
People were murdered, and pillaged, and plundered,
   Who dared but to speak in defense of the truth.

The carnage continued and spread far and wide,
   And innocent victims by thousands were slain,
When Truth from her slumber arose in her pride,
   And came forth to battle for freedom again.
But Ignorance, Error and Falsehood combined,
   And Truth was led captive and strongly enchained;
While dark Superstition, benighted and blind,
   Over Reason and Progress triumphantly reigned.

Souls must be taught to accept with contrition,
   Their unhallowed prayers, and their comfortless
Else be consigned to eternal perdition,   [faith,
   And suffer the pains of a torturing death.
Kindled were torches of vile persecution,
   Till light from their fires emblazoned the sky;
    Their dungeons and dens of pollution
     cast their poor victims to suffer and die.

What a beautiful god to love and adore,
  The one whom these tyrants for us did create,
In vain would the sinner for mercy implore,
  Before such a monster of vengeance and hate.
Against such a god loving Nature protests;
  A god so vindictive men cannot obey:
What comfort to mortals by burdens oppressed,
  To kneel to such monster and fervently pray!

Truth rising again her bright banner unfurled,
  And cast off the fetters which held her enchained;
In splendor she came to enlighten the world,
  And scatter the clouds from the mental domain.
Black was the sky in her line of procession,
  And great was the gloom in her pathway that lay;
Onward she keeps in her march of progression,
  And darkness is rapidly passing away.

So great were the clouds that enveloped the mind;
  So dense was the fog that enshrouded the brain,
That conscience was stifled and reason was blind,
  And light was expelled from the mental domain.
But Truth still advancing kept steadily on,
  Till bigots no longer her march could delay,
And soon from the mind will the cobwebs be gone,
  And Reason stand forth in the sunlight of day.

But orthodox preachers of every sect,
  Still think all are damned who are not of their fold,
And though in their speech they are more circumspect,
  They're almost as bad as the tyrants of old.
Eternal damnation to sinners they preach,
  And threaten poor souls with a terrible rod;
That hell still exists they continue to teach,
  Prepared for the lost by a merciful God.

They all disagree as to what they believe,
   But each still contends that their doctine is right,
And those whom their teaching decline to receive,
   They doom to despair in the regions of night.
They think less of truth than dogmas and creeds,
   And look upon Reason as something obscene,
In blindness they follow where bigotry leads,
   Far, far from the paths of the good Nazarene.

What with their quarreling and endless dissensions,
   How *this* one by *that* one's denounced and decried;
What with their wrangling and hateful contentions,
   How can a poor sinner between them decide?
They whom the Lord hath divinely appointed,
   The gospel to preach and the scriptures construe,
When they have become so badly disjointed,
   What then in God's name are poor mortals to do?

Do what the God of creation intended;
   Be guided by Reason and do what is right;
Let error be crushed and truth be defended,
   And open the mind to the coming of light.
Drink of the waters continually flowing
   From fountains of truth as they spring from above;
Learn what the tablets of nature are showing,
   That God is a father of infinite love.

Tho' preachers may rave and their pulpits may pound,
   And hurl at poor sinners their phials of wrath,
Yet Truth with bright garlands will shortly be crowned,
   And falsehood and error must flee from her path.
See her advancing with glory surrounded,
   To lighten all nations from center to pole,
Hail her with gladness, let joy be unbounded,
   And cursed be the wretch who would fetter the soul.

A VOICE FROM PAINE.

Hear me, ye mortals, once again,
  And hearken to the voice of Paine,
Whom those to-day who truth deny,
  Denounce, defame, and villify.
Though priests their poisoned arrows fling,
  And fools to superstition cling;
Though Error may the Right assail,
  Eternal truth shall still prevail.

Unchain the mind, unbind the soul,
  Let spirit life and truth control;
Dash down dark Superstition's wall,
  And break the fetters that enthral;
Admit the light of liberty,
  And let immortal thought be free;
No fetters forged, or chains forsooth,
  Can stay the onward march of truth.

Envenomed tongues of Orthodox,
  May fulminate to frighten flocks,
And hurl from warped, distorted brain,
  Vile curses on the head of Paine.
The seed of truth he left behind,
  Found resting place in human mind,
And there 'twill grow, like healthy tree,
  Till all mankind are conscience free.

Ye despots whom the world control,
　Dost think thou canst enchain the soul?
Or stop its onward, higher course,
　Impelled by truth and spirit force?
As well attempt from thought to flee,
　Or stop the motion of the sea;
Or undertake by force of will,
　To move the solid, rock-bound hill.

Truth for a time may bleeding lie,
　But it can never, never die;
Defying vile oppression's chain,
　On freedom's wings 'twill rise again.
The time is coming on apace,
　When Truth shall reign in Error's place;
When men will dogmas cast aside,
　And "Common Sense" shall be their guide.

Men will not always strive in vain,
　To free themselves from tyrant's chain;
Nor will their souls much longer feed
　On doctrine false and senseless creed.
Despite the theologians howl;
　Despite the monk's ferocious scowl;
O'er papal bulls and monarch's threat,
　Eternal truth shall conquer yet.

Within the church there's scarcely space,
　Where truth can show her smiling face;
But falsehood mounts the holy stair,
　Denounces Paine, and offers prayer.
Benighted mortals, why despise
　The truths that Nature still supplies?
Why choose the bad, reject the good,
　Ye offspring of one Fatherhood?

The surpliced priest, so much becrossed,
  Considers ev'ry mortal lost,
Who will not bow in humbleness
  And all his carnal sins confess;
Those who with him dare disagree,
  Are lost for all eternity;
Their souls, unshriven, down must go
  To regions of eternal woe.

Sects orthodox are all the same,
  Though each has its peculiar name;
Their doctrine to be false assume,
  And hell will be thy final doom.
Since neither's good, none can be best,
  But Calvin's worse than all the rest;
His sect believes that hell is crammed
  With infants born but to be damned.

How long will mortals blindly grope,
  To error chained, shut out from hope?
Roll up the curtains of the mind,
  That spirit light and truth may shine;
Submit not to despotic rule
  Of tyrant church or mitred fool;
Cast off the shackles, break the rod,
  Immortal soul is part of God.

Throughout the world the truth proclaim,
  Till all mankind shall know the same;
From shore to shore send forth the cry,
  That truth eternal cannot die.
Though churches fall and go to dust;
  Though falsehood die, as die it must;
Truth, springing from eternal source,
  Shall still pursue her onward course.

Be slaves no more to senseless creeds;
   Nor follow more where falsehood leads,
Tear up the roots by bigots spread,
   And plant the seed of truth instead;
Unfold the mind to spirit light,
   And learn to read with spirit sight;
Dark superstition's reign is past,
   And "Age of Reason's" come at last.

To all mankind this message send:—
   The brave are they whom truth defend;
And let the conscience-coward slave,
   Descend into dishonored grave
Be brave to do, be bold to dare,
   And strike at falsehood ev'rywhere;
Let Error from the throne be hurled,
   And Truth, triumphant, rule the world.

THE BROTHERHOOD OF MAN.

O would that men, could comprehend,
　　How each to each is brother;
Then love divine, would them entwine,
　　And bind them to each other.

From mother earth, we all had birth
　　King, potentate, and pauper;
The fruit are we, of one great tree,
　　Though some don't think it proper.

One common air, we all must share,
　　'Like on all the rains descend;
And as we run, the self-same sun,
　　Lights our pathway to the end.

Death comes to all, both great and small,
　　Rich and poor, and high and low;
The whistle calls, the curtain falls,
　　Then in silence we must go.

The lofty born, may look with scorn
　　Upon the sons of labor;
But vain is he, who claims to be
　　Much better than his neighbor.

In all his days, man only plays
　　The part for him intended;
Each bears his load, along the road,
　　Until life's journey's ended.

Some reach by flights, stupendous heights,
   All unmindful as they go,
That those who fly so very high,
   Often fall extremely low.

From brother's trip or sinful slip,
   We should derive no pleasure;
But lend a hand, whene'er we can,
   According to our measure.

For we, as they, may fall some day,
   However high our station;
A siren's glance, a slip by chance,
   May work our ruination.

It is a fact, from folly's act,
   There's none that is exempted;
And high and low, where'er they go,
   Are subject to be tempted. .

The proud of heart, who keep apart,
   And think themselves annointed;
May learn some day, they are but clay,
   And thus be disappointed.

We all some day, may go astray,
   For man is only human;
And this of course, with equal force,
   Applies as well to woman.

God does not care, how soon we share,
   The burdens of each other;
No fault he'll find, if we're inclined,
   To help a sinking brother.

And as for hell, of which some tell,
    I hold to this contention:
That no such place, for sinful race,
    Was ever God's invention.

And those who rant, with pious cant,
    And sanctimonious frothing,
May. soon or late, find they but prate,
    Of which they know but nothing.

Let all men be, but conscience free,
    Untrammelled and unfettered;
And men would find, the human kind,
    Would then be greatly bettered.

The lion caged becomes enraged,
    And furious in his wrath;
And waters pent, once given vent,
    Are dangerous in their path.

Thus man should be at liberty;
    No claim his soul should fetter;
Like river free, that seeks the sea,
    The less he's damned the better.

Men have no need, for book or creed,
    That teaches their damnation;
For they can trace, on nature's face
    God's love for all creation.

His love divine, doth brightly shine,
    And calls forth adoration;
And as we gaze, we render praise,
    In rev'rent contemplation.

We see his hand, on sea and land;
   In myriad lamps above us;
And learn to know, from things below,
   How dearly He doth love us.

The winter's snow, the summer's glow,
   The warblers sweetly singing;
The dew-drop bright, the stars at night,
   The daisies upward springing;

The murm'ring stream, the dawn's first gleam,
   The shades of twilight falling;
The smiling vale, the lovely dale,
   And cushats fondly calling;

The mountains high, the azure sky,
   The balmy laden breezes;
The flow'ry dell, the mossy fell,
   And ev'rything that pleases;

The gentle dove, the mother's love,
   The child's angelic features,
Proclaim abroad, the love of God
   For all His human creatures.

Then why should we, not brothers be,
   And loving to each other?
And ready stand, with helping hand,
   To lift a fallen brother?

We have been told, of streets of gold,
   And land that's always sunny;
Where we may rest, supremely blest,
   And live on milk and honey.

But love is meat, that's sweet to eat,
   Unequaled in its fineness;
And sweet we know, the streams that flow,
   From founts of human kindness.

The time draws nigh, to say good bye,
   To sorrow, tears, and laughter;
And those we leave, to mourn and grieve,
   Will shortly follow after.

Don't weep and moan, and sigh and groan,
   Thinking that thy soul is lost;
There is no gloom beyond the tomb,
   Once the silent stream is crossed.

WHO KNOWS?

In all creation's wondrous plan,
   What is more wonderful than man?
And who, of all the human kind,
   Can say for what he was designed?
            Who knows?

Why some are short, and others tall;
   Why some are large, and others small;
Why some are dark, and others light,
   And some as black as shades of night;
            Who knows?

Why some are fair and fine to see,
   And others coarse as coarse can be;
Why *this* one has such charming grace,
   And *that* one such repulsive face,
        Who knows?

And there are men we sometimes meet,
   In perfect form from head to feet;
But oft we see a dwarfish clod—
   Which of them most resembles God?
        Who knows?

If in God's image we are made,
   As it so often hath been said,
Then of the countless human host,
   Whose features represent him most,
        Who knows?

Is it in form we likeness bear,
   To Him that's present ev'rywhere?
Or do we image in the mind,
   The God by whom we were designed?
        Who knows?

Is there a man in truth may claim,
   To know from whence or how he came;
Or where, in all the human race,
   Is found the soul's abiding place;
        Who knows?

Of all mankind, both great and small,
   Who knows he has a soul at all?
Or who can touch the spot and swear,
   That soul immortal's centered there;
        Who knows?

Who knows there is a future life,
  Beyond this vale of tears and strife?
Or that, when comes the final call,
  Death is, or not, the end of all,
        Who knows?

Was Adam, of the human race,
  The first on earth to find a place?
Or for ten thousand years and more,
  Did not the race exist before?
        Who knows?

Who knows the cause, in truth and fact,
  Of Adam's disobedient act;
Or whether he should Eve have known,
  Had he the apple let alone,
        Who knows?

Who knows, when Abel had been slain,
  And murdered by his brother Cain,
The kind of mark Cain had to bear,
  That men might know him ev'rywhere?
        Who knows?

If Adam, Eve, and Cain were all
  Who peopled then this earthly ball,
How was it Cain could go abroad,
  And take a wife in land of Nod?
        Who knows?

When Moses with his murd'rous hand,
  Egyptian slew upon the sand,
He thought, perhaps, he need not run,
  As no one saw what he had done,
        Who knows?

Next day what made him take to flight,
   When asked by wrothful Israelite,
"What mean'st thou, sir, would'st thou me slay,
   As did'st Egyptian yesterday?"
         Who knows?

Was it by God's direct command,
   He fled so fast from Phar'oh's land?
Or was it not a guilty fear
   That made him run and disappear?
         Who knows?

When Moses viewed from Pisgah's height,
   The land of promise and delight,
Was he translated there and then,
   Or did he die like other men?
         Who knows?

And as to that most wondrous tale,
   Of Jonah swallowed by the whale,
How did he manage while afloat,
   To glide so smoothly down his throat?
         Who knows?

No doubt the monster of the deep
   Was sometime troubled in his sleep,
By Jonah tramping 'round about,
   In search of some place to get out,
         Who knows?

The whale kept swimming thro' the tide,
   With Jonah safely lodged inside;
At length for shore he made a break,
   Perhaps impelled by stomach-ache,
         Who knows?

As soon as he had reached the land,
   And stretched himself upon the sand,
He felt some griping pains, no doubt,
   Which made him throw poor Jonah out,
       Who knows?

Before the walls of Jericho,
   The trumpeters did loudly blow;
Was it the sound of trumpet call,
   That caused the walls to shake and fall?
       Who knows?

How did it ever come to pass
   That David, lustful as he was,
Should be, of all men, set apart
   As being after God's own heart?
       Who knows?

As Balaam, mounted on his ass,
   Approached a narrow mountain pass,
By what strange cause, or what strange freak,
   The donkey as a man could speak?
       Who knows?

Can virgin pure, to man unknown,
   Conceive and bring forth child alone?
If such a thing can not be done,
   Then how could Mary have a son?
       Who knows?

If Christ was not the son of man,
   But lived before the world began,
And *was* the son of the Divine,
   How could He be of David's line?
       Who knows?

And is there, as the preachers say,
   A place of everlasting day,
Where those who are from sin set free,
   May dwell through all eternity?
          Who knows?

Is heav'n a place by God designed,
   Or but creation of the mind?
Is it in form a plane or ball,
   Or is there such a place at all,
          Who knows?

The other place of which they tell,
   And which they designate as hell,
Where unredeemed must tortures bear,
   Does it exist, and, if so, where!
          Who knows? .

Take all the doctrines preached to-day,
   To draw men to the narrow way,
From gospel Old, or gospel New,
   And which is false and which is true,
          Who knows?

At last, when we have run our race,
   And sleep in death's long, cold embrace,
Where shall the soul immortal be
   Throughout the long eternity,
          Who knows?

Since none may say where it shall go,
   To heav'n above or hell below,
Trust Him who brought us from the past,
   To say where we shall go at last,
          He knows.

TRUTH.

Hail, glorious Truth! Ascending star,
　By priests and bigots long suppressed,
Once more in triumph thou dost rise,
　Like eagle tow'ring from her nest.

Kings and priests no longer bind thee,
　And torture thee on cruel rack;
Tyrants tremble at thy coming
　And vainly strive to beat thee back.

Superstition flies before thee,
　And bigots gaze in wild dismay,
Whilst thou leadest souls from darkness
　To light of everlasting day.

Clouds disperse before thy coming,
　And fettered souls from bondage rise;
Those who groped their way in blindness
　Have had the scales struck from their eyes.

Brazen Falsehood, long triumphant,
　Like thief who fears to face the light,
Or like coward in the battle,
　Attempts to save itself by flight.

Fear and Terror have been vanquished,
　And Error from her throne is hurled;
Truth, in triumph, is advancing,
　And soon will circumvent the world.

Creeds and Dogmas, tyrants' weapons,
   Bulwarks of sanctimon'ous fraud,
Are crumbling 'neath the strokes of those
   Whose creed is Truth, whose trust is God.

Stead'ly on thy march continue,
   Thy banner keep aloft unfurled;
Sound the glorious proclamation,
   That Truth has come to rule the world.

NUMBER ONE.

Let preachers preach and thinkers think,
   And men philosophise;
Let ranters bellow till they're hoarse
   Of homes beyond the skies;
But mortals better be content
   With homes not quite so high,
Than undertake to soar aloft
   To mansions in the sky.

It may be well to place our hopes
   Upon the golden shore,
And think of crowns that wait for us
   When earthly toil is o'er;
But while upon this mundane sphere,
   We'd better, if we can,
Accumulate some worldly goods
   And think of Number One.

We cannot soar without the wings
 To homes so very high;
And earthly homes are good enough
 For those who cannot fly;
And though the preachers caution us
 That life is but a span;
They take advantage of the time,
 And think of Number One.

They do not care to trust alone
 To treasures over There;
But strive as other mortals do
 To get a worldly share;
And while they shout their songs of praise
 And preach salvation's free,
They always like to get the church,
 That pays the largest fee.

Prayers in their place are good enough,
 And so is preaching too,
But if we get but spirit food
 What will the body do?
The stomach craves for something else,
 And wise will be the man,
Who hearkens to the stomach's voice
 And thinks of Number One.

The hungry soul the preacher would
 With gospel feed and cram,
But for the body famishing
 He does not care a d——n;
He thinks by preaching and by prayer
 The hungry may be fed,
But will not give a five-cent piece
 To buy a loaf of bread.

But doubtless there may still be found
   A few among the whole,
Who think a loaf of bread or two
   Might sometimes help the soul.
But these are not of Orthodox
   Or Calvanistic school,
But are, by kindly deeds performed,
   Exceptions to the rule.

Friendship will do to talk about,
   But that has metes and bounds,
Its measurement, when at its best,
   Is shillings, pence, and pounds;
And men may say just what they please,
   'Tis much the better plan,
To waste no time upon our friends
   But think of Number One.

The pearly gates and shining streets,
   And homes so bright and fair,
Are beautiful, no doubt, to those
   Who've climbed the golden stair;
But since old Adam ate the fruit,
   When first the world began,
Those men have always thrived the best
   Who thought of Number One.

AT PETER'S GATE.

A knock was heard at Peter's gate,
　"Who's there?" the saint replied,
"The spirit of a millionaire
　Just from the other side."

"What seek'st thou here?" quoth Peter then,
　"That thou com'st knocking so?
Dost think the same rules here apply,
　That govern down below?"

"Here no distinction's ever made
　'Tween high and low estate;
The beggar and the millionaire
　Stand equal at the gate."

'Good Peter, pray thee, let me in,
　Withhold not thy consent;
For any wrong I may have done,
　Sincerely I repent.

"Such cannot be," good Peter said,
　"There's no repentance here;
If thou didst not repent before,
　'Tis rather late I fear."

"But let me hear how thou hast lived;
　There may be still a chance,
And if I find thy claim is good,
　I'll ope the gate at once."

On hearing what the Saint had said,
 The spirit thus began:—
"My greed for wealth drove from my heart,
 All love for fellowman."

"On riches all my thoughts were placed,
 I dreamt of them by night,
And millions to accumulate
 Became my chief delight."

"I gambled much in stocks and bonds;
 I dealt in railway shares;
And many were the traps I set
 To catch the "bulls" and "bears.""

"The market oft I have depressed
 To make the prices fall,
And oft, my plans to execute,
 Drove many to the wall."

"I never played the cards to lose,
 Of that you may be sure,
And treasures to my coffers came,
 Alike from rich and poor.'"

"I practised all the tricks of trade,
 To move, to feint, to draw,
And though my methods were condemned
 I kept within the law."

"Few were the moves I ever made
 But that increased my store,
And though I many millions gained,
 Yet still I grasped for more."

"But, to my shame, I must confess,
  I played a miser's part,
And as I saw my riches grow.
  More callous grew my heart."

"At length my health began to fail,
  Death followed sure and fast,
And all the millions that were mine
  I had to leave at last."

"I nothing left to aid the poor,
  But that was not a sin;
And ev'ry dollar I possessed
  Went to my kith and kin."

"My explanation closes here,
  No more have I to state,
And now you surely won't object
  To pass me through the gate."

Then Peter thus:—"Thy truthfulness
  I have no cause to doubt,
But my respect for those within
  Will make me keep thee out."

"Though there are many mansions here,
  And all provided free,
I do not think in all the realm
  There's one prepared for thee."

"That mortals should not riches gain,
  Is not the law's decree;
But in the Book there are commands
  To deeds of charity."

"How many naked have you clothed?
   How many hungry fed?
How many starving little ones
   Have you supplied with bread?"

"How many in the name of Christ
   Have ever you received?
How many needy, suff'ring souls
   Have ever you relieved?"

"How many orphans have you cheered
   By either word or deed?
How many widows have you helped
   In time of sorest need?"

"How many of your fellowmen
   Had ever cause to say,
"God bless you" for your kindly acts,
   When they knelt down to pray?"

"For those in deep affliction cast,
   What hast thou ever done?
What homes for helpless have you built?
   You have not mentioned one."

"How many deeds of charity
   Didst thou find time to do?
How many blessings of the poor
   Have ever followed you?"

"Although the treasures of the earth
   By millions to you came;
To thirsty soul you never gave
   Cold water in His name."

"Not all the millions you possessed
    Can aid you in your need;
You gained the wealth but lost your soul,
    By avarice and greed."

"Begone," said Peter, "from the gate,
    Thy steps you must retrace,
You can not be admitted here,
    Go try the other place."

JIM.

A kinder heart than his ne'er beat
    Within a human breast;
No hand more ready to relieve
    The suff'ring and distressed;
He always gave of what he had,
    It mattered not to him;
And when he gave, the smaller part
    Was always left with Jim.

He cared not what the color was
    Of those who sought his aid;
One brotherhood embraced them all,
    No matter what their shade;
Nor did he question what the creed
    Of those who came to him;
And whether they were Jew or Greek
    'Twas all the same to Jim.

He did not always have the means
  To do with as he would,
But still with those at his command
  He did the best he could;
He gave from promptings of the heart,
  And not from any whim;
And those he could not aid when asked,
  Felt not so bad as Jim.

If ever friend to him would go,
  And tale of woe relate,
He got whatever he possessed,
  However small or great;
And much or little though he had,
  It made no change in him;
He still remained, and still was found
  The same kind-hearted Jim.

He never saw a little lad
  Look hungry on the street,
But that he slipped into his hand
  The price of food to eat;
And when old age to him would plead
  With feeble tott'ring limb,
It always found a ready hand
  And gen'rous friend in Jim.

Sometimes his friends would say to him,
  He yet might see the day
When he most sadly would regret
  He gave so much away;
But he would tell them with a smile,
  The fault was not with him;
If nature made him what he was
  The blame was not with Jim.

Some thought he had peculiar ways,
   And classed him as a fool;
But those were they who nothing knew
   About the "Golden Rule;"
Not as my neighbor does to me
   Should I do unto him;
But as I *would* that he should do
   Was still the rule for Jim.

But yet for all his kindly deeds,
   Jim had his faults, 'tis true,
And some might think the faults he had
   Were far from being few;
But yet whate'er they pleased to think
   Or choose to say of him;
The greatest fault to charge him with
   Was his neglect of Jim.

The thoughts he thought he freely spoke,
   No matter where he stood;
And if convinced that he was right,
   Would face a multitude;
And never creature in distress
   That would appeal to him,
But would receive, had he the means,
   A helping hand from Jim.

Some thought he was chimerical,
   Inclined to always stray,
And soar aloft on Fancy's wings
   To regions far away;
But others thought quite otherwise
   And highly spoke of him,
And only wished the world had more
   Like tender-hearted Jim.

As regarded things religious,
   He was lib'ral in his views;
But did not think that all were saints
   Who sat in cushioned pews;
He thought God knew his business
   And left it all with Him;
And those who preached eternal hell
   Might have it all for Jim.

But years crept on and he grew old,
   His hair got white as snow,
And all the children welcomed him
   Wherever he would go;
They'd gather round in little groups
   And cluster close to him,
Delighted all to hear a tale
   From good old Grandpa Jim.

At length one day to him there came
   A summons loud and clear,
And soldier-like he did respond
   And faintly answered, "Here;"
Then turned his eyes on those around,
   With vision faint and dim,
And feebly said, "God bless you all,
   Here goes the last of Jim."

SPIRIT VOICES.

Hark!   I hear sweet voices humming,
   Humming softly through the air,
And I see bright faces coming
   From the regions over There;
Voices humming, faces coming,
   Smiling faces bright and fair,
Coming, coming, nearer coming,
   Gliding gently through the air.

Loving faces, long departed,
   Come to greet us from above,
To the wounded, aching hearted,
   Bringing messages of love.
Arms extending, voices blending,
   Singing sweetly through the air,
Yonder, Yonder, over Yonder,
   No more pain or sorrow there.

Now advancing, now receding,
   Constantly they come and go,
Spirit-voices ever pleading
   With the loved ones here below;
Hear those sweet, delightful voices
   Floating downward from above,
Singing, singing, sweetly singing,
   Songs of endless joy and love.

MOTHER'S GRAVE.

Of all the earth, this little spot
   To me more sacred is than all;
'Tis here my mother's ashes rest,
   Whose loving face I still recall.
I've strayed along the Bosphor's banks,
   And walked by Como's rippling wave,
But never have I seen the spot,
   So dear to me as mother's grave.

I will remember that sad day,
   As here I stood with grief oppressed,
And wept as though my heart would break,
   As she was laid away to rest.
Through all my pilgrimage of life,
   I earnestly this boon did crave:
That God would lengthen out my days
   Till I should see my mother's grave.

Then I was only but a lad,
   But great the loss I had to bear;
For who can take a mother's place,
   And give the child such loving care?
But God has spared me, bless His name,
   Through dangers great on land and wave,
And here, once more, at three-score years,
   I stand beside my mother's grave.

As on the tented field I've lain,
   And watched the stars so bright and clear,
From blissful realms that lay beyond,
   Would come the form of mother dear;
And as I looked upon her face,
   And saw the tender smile she gave,
On wings of thought I would be borne,
   And placed beside my mother's grave.

And as in battle I have stood,
   With Death's grim visage standing near,
As angel bright, with outstretched wings,
   Would mother's face to me appear.
And as my comrades all around,
   Fell thick and fast, like heroes brave,
Amidst the scenes of carnage there,
   My thoughts would fly to mother's grave.

I know there's nothing now but dust
   Beneath this grassy little mound;
But not for worlds would I exchange
   This little spot of hallowed ground.
The tombstone's crumbling to decay,
   Time, in its march, will nothing save,
But still the name engraved thereon,
   Tells me that this is mother's grave.

Death now must shortly come to me,
   But still I have abiding trust,
And only wish when comes the end,
   To mingle with this sacred dust.
I've traveled full three thousand miles,
   Across deep ocean's briny wave,
And here I render thanks to God,
   For bringing me to mother's grave.

THE WORLD WE LIVE IN.

What a world is this we live in!
  How varied are the scenes of life!
There are days of pain and pleasure,
  And also days of broil and strife;
Days of anguish, days of gladness,
  Swell into months, and months to years;
Days of labor, toil, and sadness,
  Days of laughter, and days of tears.

Days of health, and days of sickness,
  Days of mis'ry, want, and woe,
Days of joy, and days of sorrow,
  Each after each they come and go.
Days of light, and days of blackness,
  And days when all seem bright and fair;
Busy days, and days of slackness,
  Days overshadowed with despair.

Days of peace, and days of trouble,
  And days of comfort and content;
Days to pleasure all devoted,
  And days in melancholy spent.
Days of aches and sore affliction,
  And days of mingling doubts and fears;
Cheerful days, days of dejection,
  All go to swell the passing years.

Days by trials sorely tested,
   And days when we temptations meet;
Days of racking self-contention,
   And days of triumph and defeat.
Days of feasting, days of fasting,
   And days of mourning too we see,
Prosp'rous days, too seldom lasting,
   And days of dire adversity.

Days of weeping, and rejoicing,
   And days when we lament our birth;
Days of pining and regretting,
   Despondent days, and days of mirth.
Days of disappointments fearful,
   Thoughtful days of sad reflection,
Days when we are bright and cheerful,
   Days of bitter retrospection.

Days in useless effort wasted,
   And days a prey to grief and care;
Festive days, and days perplexing,
   Days "building castles in the air."
Days of lofty aspirations,
   And days of discontent and gloom,
Each, and all, are only stations,
   Between the cradle and the tomb.

Those there are whose fare is princely,
   And those whose picking is but scant;
Some who live in regal splendor,
   And some in penury and want.
Some go robed in silks and laces,
   While some in rags and tatters go;
Some reside in costly places,
   While others dwell in hovels low.

Some there are who ride in coaches,
  While others plod along on foot;
Some who wear the finest calfskin.
  While some have neither shoe nor boot.
Some eat the best that can be found,
  While others beg from door to door;
Some sleep on beds of softest down,
  While others have to take the floor.

Hearts with hope are loudly beating,
  While other hearts but sob and sigh;
Hearts for joy are madly bounding,
  While others wounded, bleeding lie·
Hearts there are in love imbedded,
  That feel for others in distress;
Hearts there are so heavy leaded.
  They sink in greed and selfishness.

Homes there are where love and duty,
  Brightens every day of life:
Homes there are where jealous hatreds,
  Engender only broil and strife.
Homes there are where no dissension,
  Disturbs or mars the peaceful sway;
Homes there are where fierce contention,
  Drives peace, and joy, and love away.

Here, 'mid the scenes of heightened joy,
  All too fast the hours are flying;
There, writhing on a bed of pain,
  Some one's darling's slowly dying.
Here, bride to groom is wed to-day,
  And merry peals the marriage bell;
There, solemn cortege wends its way,
  And doleful sounds the fun'ral knell.

Thus while sailing on Life's ocean,
  Forever changing is the scene,
Billows rise in wild commotion,
  With waves of peace and calm between.
But past them all we're gliding on,
  Fast sailing toward Eternity,
And soon we'll reach the great Beyond,
  The realms of Hope and Mystery.

DEAR OLD NATIVE HOME.

I love my dear old native home,
  Though 'twas a little cot;
The happy days enjoyed therein,
  Shall never be forgot;
I left it many years ago,
  And sailed across the sea.
But still! I yearn to see once more,
  The home so dear to me.

Though I enjoy the blessings here,
  That freedom doth impart;
Yet I can see a little cot,
  That's still dear to my heart.
Though comforts great are mine to share,
  My thoughts still love to roam.
Back to the spot where I was born,
  The dear old native home.

It was there my mother taught me,
　　The Lord's prayer to repeat,
As tenderly she stroked my head,
　　Whilst kneeling at her feet;
And there she pointed out to me,
　　The paths the righteous trod;
And taught me in my youthful days,
　　To love and fear my God.

Each morn and eve we gathered round,
　　The fam'ly altar there,
To offer up our praise to God,
　　And humbly kneel in prayer;
In turn we read the Holy Book,
　　While father would preside,
Who taught us that the Word of God,
　　Should always be our guide.

And thus within t'rat little cot,
　　Year after year passed by,
Each bringing peace and happiness,
　　And blessings from on High.
The cot was small, a "butt" and "ben,"
　　Comprised its chiefest parts,
And though the roof was made of thatch,
　　It sheltered happy hearts.

No carpet for our feet was spread;
　　A latch string closed the door;
But yet we had some pleasant times,
　　Upon the earthen floor.
Our music was the violin,
　　And brother John would play;
While "Annie Laurie" we would sing,
　　Or grand old "Scots Wha Hae."

The income that supported us,
  Was rather small, 'tis true,
But yet to compensate for this,
  Our wants were very few;
Though void of ev'ry luxury,
  The table still was spread,
Industrious hands and honest toil,
  Still furnished daily bread.

Our Sunday clothes were nothing more,
  Than corduroy and plaid;
But yet we always went to church,
  Content with what we had.
The sermon sounded just as good;
  The heartfelt offered prayer,
Would reach our hearts as soon, perhaps,
  As many others there.

Whatever now that I possess,
  Of goodness and of truth,
Were there, within that little cot,
  Implanted in my youth.
What wonder then, though far away,
  My thoughts still love to roam,
Back to the spot where I was born,
  The dear old native home.

THE DYING MARINER.

When I shall die I wish to lie
    Close by the ocean deep,
Where silv'ry wave can wash my grave—
    'Tis there I wish to sleep.
No mournful strain or sad refrain
    Sing o'er my peaceful grave;
The swelling surge shall chant my dirge,
    Down by the deep blue wave.

I loved to ride deep ocean's tide
    And scud before the gale,
And watch the spray as it would play
    Around the snow-white sail.
My barque and crew were stanch and true
    As ever mounted wave,
And by the sea I roamed so free
    Is where I wish my grave.

I near the shore where nevermore
    I'll sail the ocean vast;
To peaceful tide I soon shall glide
    And there my anchor cast;
For mass or prayer I do not care
    To waft me on the way,
In Him I trust, the Good and Just,
    Whom wind and waves obey.

But I would sleep by ocean deep,
  Close by the rolling sea,
Where waves might lave my silent grave
  And murmur still to me.
The shore is reached, my barque is beached,
  The voyage now is o'er,
And safe at last my anchor's cast
  Where I shall drift no more.

ON THE DEATH OF A CHILD.

Sweet cherub. Wesley, my first-born,
  Here by thy side I sit and weep,
And O, how my sad heart is torn.
  To see thee lie in death's cold sleep.

Thy angel face, so fair to see,
  On which the sweet departing smile
Still loves to rest; and which to me
  Was ever joy. My child, My child!

Death hath snatched thee from my embrace,
  And filled thy mother's heart with woe;
No more upon thy cherub face,
  I'll see the sweet smile come and go.

And as I gaze in my despair,
  On thee my child, departed joy;
I offer up a mother's prayer,
  To meet again my darling boy.

But O, 'tis hard to part with thee,
   And to the grave thy form consign,
To know thy face no more I'll see,
   Nor press again thy lips to mine.

On thy cold lips I'll now bestow,
   A mother's parting kiss of love,
And wait till I am called to go,
   To meet thee, darling, up above.

Farewell, my child.   I mourn thy loss,
   But meekly bow beneath the rod,
And prayerfully take up my cross,
   And say, "Thy will be done" O, God.

AN OUTRAGED WOMAN'S CURSE.

Thou hateful wretch, again we meet,
   And for this meeting I have longed;
Here, ruined by thy damned deceit,
   Behold the woman thou hast wronged.

You shun me now, thou hell-born wretch,
   As something that you can't endure;
Forgetful of the time when I
   Was chaste and spotless, young and pure.

You then avowed eternal faith,
   And I believed your faithless vow;
My very heart and soul were thine,
   And for my love, behold me now.

Behold the ruin thou hast made,
　For which, be damned thy lying heart;
Strike, scoundrel, strike me if you dare,
　I fear thee not, wretch that thou art.

Yes, tremble fiend, for well you may,
　My wrongs demand avenging hand;
Could I but send thy soul to hell,
　I'd blast you, scoundrel, where you stand.

My ev'ry hope in life you crushed,
　You left me spoiled and desolate,
And all the love I bore thee once,
　But now intensifies my hate.

I had a home, a happy home,
　Whose threshold vice had never crossed;
The love of parents once was mine,
　But all are now forever lost.

I once had friends, but even they,
　Now loathe and hate my very name;
Of all the joys that once were mine,
　There's nothing left me now but shame.

You made the wreck, accursed wretch,
　And now you beg me to be calm;
You drove me from my peaceful home,
　'Twas you that made me what I am.

You spurn me now, and cast me off;
　The shame is borne alone by me;
But know an outraged woman's curse,
　Henceforth shall ever follow thee.

May curses rest on thee and thine;
   May foul diseases fall on thee;
I curse thee now, and be thou curst,
   Through time and through eternity.

If ever wife fall to thy lot,
   May she forever childless be;
If ever child to thee is born,
   Be it a thwart and curse to thee.

And for the home that once was mine,
   And for the tears my mother shed,
And for my father's broken heart,
   May curses fall upon thy head.

I curse thee for my virtue lost,
   I curse thee for the shame I bear;
An unwed mother curses thee,
   And bids thy guilty soul despair.

May cancer gnaw thy faithless heart;
   May ev'ry ill that's man's to share,
And ev'ry pain to mortals known,
   But all increased, be thine to bear.

I curse thee from my ruined soul,
   May curses follow thee till death;
For what I am, for what I've borne,
   I'll curse thee with my dying breath.

TO A ROSE.

Sweet blooming rose, how fair thou art,
   How beautiful thou art to see,
But soon thy beauty may depart,
   And then what will become of thee?

Perhaps, like me, thou'rt doomed to fall,
   And perish 'neath some wretch's clutch,
And thou wilt then, when lost to all,
   Be deemed too vile for man to touch.

And when thy ruin is complete,
   And all thy charms forever gone,
Then thou'lt be thrown into the street,
   For heartless men to tread upon.

Not long ago I bloomed like thee,
   With beauty's impress on my brow,
But blighting hand soon fell on me,
   And I became what I am now.

And what I am thou soon may'st be,
   A worthless thing to be passed by,
Despised by all humanity,
   And left to wither, fade, and die.

Could'st thou be always fair to see,
   Thou'dst meet with tender kiss and smile,
But once thy charms are gone from thee,
   Thou'lt then be loathed as something vile.

Could'st thou thy beauty but conceal,
    And hide thy sweet and charming face,
Thou might'st escape what now I feel,
    And die at last without disgrace.

When I was young and bloomed like thee,
    How many sought my heart to win,
But when I lost my purity,
    Then I was called a child of sin.

When I to vice and shame was cast,
    No helping hand was stretched to me,
And virtue scoffed me as she passed,
    She would not aid a wretch like me.

And now, wherever I appear,
    There's no one that will take me in;
These taunting words I ever hear:
    "Be off, be off, you child of sin."

Had Nature not adorned my face,
    And Beauty left its impress there,
I would not now be lost to grace,
    Nor suffer what I have to bear.

And were it thine, sweet rose, to be
    Bereft those charms which thee adorn,
Thou might'st bloom on in purity,
    For who would think to pluck the thorn.

Thy beauty only renders thee
    To some designing wretch a prey,
Who, when he spoils thy chastity,
    Will rudely fling thee then away.

Sweet lips may kiss thy blushing face,
    And fond caresses may be thine,
Until another takes thy place;
    When thou shalt share a fate like mine.

Deserted, fallen, world betossed,
    Despised alike by friends and foes,
Despoiled and spurned, forever lost,
    My blooming, sweet, and charming rose.

VICTORIA.

Victoria, thou Queen of Queens,
    Of Monarchs thou art gem;
A nobler head was ne'er adorned
    With royal diadem;
Queen of good old Merry England,
    The brightest spot on earth,
Where liberty still loves to dwell,
    And freedom first found birth.

The scepter that by thee is borne
    A gentle hand doth move;
The tenderness that marks thy rule
    Calls forth thy subjects love;
Though England's crown on thee is placed,
    And Empress too you be,
The people carry in their hearts
    A brighter crown for thee.

Nor does the little sea-girt isle
    That sits the seas between,
Contain the hearts of all who love
    Great Britain's noble Queen;
For here in great America,
    Proud empire of the West,
Of all the monarchs of the earth
    Thy name is loved the best.

Nor art thou loved because **thou art**
    Of royal pedigree;
Nor yet because thou art enthroned
    In robes of majesty;
No, not for these in freemen's hearts
    Hast thy name found a shrine,
But for the matchless purity
    And virtues that art thine.

Not all the monarchs that have reigned
    On England's mighty throne,
Have brought such lustre to the crown
    As that by thee alone;
Nor is it to be wondered at
    That such should be the case,
Since thou so richly art endowed
    By Nature for the place.

No monarch ever sat a throne
    So well beloved as thee;
No subjects ever served a King
    With such fidelity;
Think not it is thy royal rank,
    Or yet thy royal blood,
That wins thee universal love
    And boundless gratitude.

'Tis not old England's regal throne
   That makes thy name adored,
For Kings and Queens have sat thereon
   Detested and abhorred;
'Tis not that thou art of the line
   Of Brunswick or of Guelph,
But for the nobler qualities
   Inborn within thyself.

One more decade, and sixty years
   Will then have passed and fled,
Since England's crown was placed upon
   Thy fair and youthful head;
And as each fleeting year passed by,
   The more thy goodness shown,
Till in thy virtues soon were lost
   The splendors of the throne.

Highly honored is the nation
   O'er which thou long hast reigned;
Its bright escutcheon 'neath thy rule,
   Hath never yet been stained;
And whilst thou ever counseled peace,
   Like ruler good and true,
Thou still didst guard thy people's rights,
   And England's honor too.

Thou hast tasted, too, of sorrow,
   But in thy widowhood,
Sweet consolation thou hast found
   In christian fortitude;
And when the loved ones whom thou lost,
   Were laid in dreamless sleep,
Thy Queenly heart then felt the grief
   That makes a mother weep.

What wonder, then, that loving hearts
   Should raise to thee a shrine;
What wonder that a nation's tears
   Should fall with those of thine;
What wonder that thy name is loved
   Wherever it is known,
The noblest Queen that ever reigned
   Or sat upon a throne.

As woman, wife, and mother too,
   In virtues unexcelled;
As ruler, blessed with qualities
   That stand unparalleled;
May many years of happiness,
   Yet still by thee be seen;
Long may'st thou reign, Victoria,
   Old England's noble Queen.

FREEDOM.

What more fondly to be cherished,
  Than pure and spotless liberty?
Wherein can man find nobler boast,
  Than in the fact that he is free?
To move and act with manly pride,
  Unfettered by the tyrant's chain,
And ever free to speak and act,
  His independence to maintain.

Not a freedom that will truckle,
  To paltry gold or titled name;
Or will bow in abject meanness,
  To gilded pomp or empty fame;
Not a freedom that will pander,
  To ev'ry rogue who chance may rule;
Or doff the hat in low submission,
  To ev'ry shining, tinselled fool.

Such freedom but excites the scorn
  Of those whose hearts are true and brave·
And he who has no higher aim,
  Is but the vilest, meanest slave.
And yet how many men there are,
  Who cringe, and bow, and bend the knee,
To some official sordid knave,
  Then loudly boast of being free.

A plague on all such truckling slaves;
  May hempen cords compress their throats;
They value freedom by the price
  That may be paid for bartered votes.
May itches seize the wretch so vile,
  Whose craven spirit cannot see,
That nothing more ennobles man,
  Than God's high gift of being free.

The man who will not fawn to wealth,
  Nor frown on honest poverty,
Nor worship at the shrine of rank,
  Nor to position bend the knee;
Whose soul no master will obey,
  Save Him who rules by right divine,
And who respects his fellowman,
  Regardless of his race or line;

Whose spirit will not brook to be,
  A slave to priest or petty lord;
Who knows no standard for a man,
  Above his principle and word;
Who spurns with contempt and with scorn,
  All claims to birth of high degree,
But measures manhood by its worth,
  'Tis his to boast of being free.

THE SOUTHERN BRIDE.

As fair was she as mellow ray,
　That gilds the sky at close of day;
Her stately form and charming face,
　A queen of loveliness might grace.
No swan that swims on stream or lake,
　Such graceful curve of neck could make
As she, when gracefully she bowed
　Responsive to the cheering crowd.

So light her step as she would pass,
　'Twould scarcely bend a blade of grass;
And when she smiled, one then could see
　A picture of divinity.
The lips would part, and just beneath,
　One caught a glimpse of pearly teeth;
A brighter line shone in her eyes,
　And dimples to her cheeks would rise.

So dignified her walk and mien,
　She looked from head to foot a queen;
And diadem can never rest
　On fairer brow than she possessed.
As diamonds sparkle in the light,
　So shone her eyes as clear and bright;
Her poise of head and cast of face,
　Were models of unequalled grace.

Hail, peerless one!   We welcome thee,
  With joy to our community;
Though cold may seem our northern parts,
  'Tis ever sunshine in our hearts.
We welcome thee with hearts sincere;
  We welcome thee with royal cheer;
We welcome thee with love and pride;
  We welcome thee thou bonnie bride.

DEATH OF SITTING BULL.

The life of the Chief has been brought to a close;
No more shall the pale-face disturb his repose;
His war-whoop is silenced, his bow is unstrung,
And nerveless the arm that the tomahawk swung.

No more shall he lead his brave followers true,
With daring and courage unequaled by few;
No more shall his arrow speed on in its flight,
As charging to meet the pale-face in the fight.

As the bold, daring huntsman, engaged in the chase,
Thinks nothing of danger, nor slackens his pace;
So rode the brave Chieftain, in war-paint adorned;
Of death he was fearless, and danger he scorned.

He breathed not his last as he hoped that he might,
In forefront of battle engaged in the fight;
He met not the death that a hero would die,
Who recked not of safety when danger was nigh.

He cared not for numbers when war was the game,
For one or ten thousand to him was the same;
No odds could deter him; and once in the field
Would fight to the death, but he never would yield.

He stood midst his foes like a king newly crowned,
And scornfully glanced at his captors around;
The flash of his eye, and the heave of his chest,
Proclaimed the wild conflict that raged in his breast.

"Ye cravens," he said, and he spoke like a king,
"Ye guard me with bayonets, and tie me with string;
I plead not for mercy, your threats I defy,
And here stands a foe who can fearlessly die."

"Think not for a moment to thee will I sue,
Or ask any mercy of cravens like you;
I would not dishonor my tribe and my race,
By bringing upon them such lasting disgrace."

"Ye look on the savage with haughty disdain,
And chase him and hunt him on mountain and plain;
But here is the truth, you have found to your woe,
The savage can fight when he meets with his foe."

"Ye stand there like cravens, all shaking with fear,
And bound as I am, yet ye dare not come near;
Base minions of power! Ye cowards and slaves!
Go bury yourselves in your dastardly graves."

"Your worst ye may do.   I have no more to say;"
And there stood the Chief like a lion at bay;
One withering glance at his captors he cast,
That spoke his defiance; that look was his last.

The hand of a coward delivered the thrust,
By which the brave Chieftain was laid in the dust;
But placed face to face, with weapon in hand,
The coward who struck would have trembled to stand.

Though captive and bound, and surrounded by foes;
Defenceless to strike or to ward off the blows;
He stood as unshaken as rock in the blast,
And proud and defiant remained to the last.

His captors might well have their cruelties ceased,
And had some respect for his courage at least;
But slight is the mercy that cowards extend,
And cravens will strike where brave men would defend.

O, shame to the country, and shame to the race,
That murder so cruel should ever take place;
And shame to the army where soldier was found,
To murder a captive when helpless and bound.

The dastard who struck such a cowardly blow,
To silence forever a valorous foe,
Had no sense of honor, of manhood, or shame,
And henceforth should *coward* be linked to his name.

When such can take place in a civilized land,
What can we expect of a wild savage band?
If such be the lesson we wish to convey,
We prove ourselves then just as savage as they.

The Chief whom they murdered, now rests' 'neath the
His fighting is ended, his spirit's with God;   [sod;
But oft in the wigwam, the red man will tell
How the pale-faces acted when Sitting Bull fell.

LYING IN THE RIVER.

Beneath the river's rippling sound,
  A man eternal rest has found;
But while the mortal part is there,
  The never-dying part is—where?

Ah, tell me, O ye orthodox,
  Who preach salvation to your flocks,
Where has it gone? Above? Below?
  Tell if thou canst, or do ye know?

Has it gone to that resting place,
  Ye say is only found through grace?
But if that grace it did not share,
  Its resting place is—tell me, where?

In hell, ye say. Why then, I must
  Believe the God ye preach unjust;
But this I can not, will not do,
  For He is love and mercy too.

Ye charge his death to God, I know,
　　And say He willed it should be so;
Thus disregarding all those laws,
　　By which effect must follow cause.

No matter what his creed was here,
　　While dwelling on this mundane sphere;
Christian, Pagan, 'tis all the same,
　　His soul's with God from whom it came.

SITTING BY THE RIVER.

Onward flows the silent river,
　　Toward the distant sea;
And onward glides my weary soul,
　　Toward eternity.
O, may its course as peaceful be,
　　Till on the golden shore,
It rests from all the toils of life,
　　In peace forevermore.

Here, all is strife, and toil, and care,
　　And pleasures are but brief;
No cup of pleasure that we drink
　　But what is mixed with grief.
There, all is peace, and joy, and love,
　　And weary souls find rest;
Here, sorrow enters ev'ry home,
　　And pierces ev'ry breast.

Here, waves of trouble never cease,
  And each succeeding roll
Brings to the heart its share of grief,
  And sorrow to the soul;
A loved one dies, some dear one falls,
  We lose some bosom friend,
And thus grief after grief succeeds,
  Until we reach the end.

Drift on my soul, the stream of life
  On which thou'rt roughly tossed,
With all its dangers and its toils,
  Will very soon be crossed;
And then adieu to earthly strife;
  Farewell to sorrow's tear;
Then onward glide my weary soul,
  The hav'n of rest is near.

GOD BLESS THE BAIRNS.

Whene'er I see a little lad,
　With feet unshod and poorly clad;
Whose little cheeks so pale and gaunt,
　Bespeak of penury and want;
Whose little eyes imploring plead,
　For aid to help him in his need;
I look at him with feelings sad,
　And can't but say—God bless the lad.

See standing there that little child,
　With cheeks so thin and eyes so mild;
Afraid to mention her distress,
　Or tell her tale of wretchedness;
None stop a kindly word to speak,
　None note the tear upon her cheek;
All pass her by with unconcern,
　Nor even say—God bless the bairn.

Poor little things! In all the throng,
　That surges by with mirth and song;
How few that look with tender eye,
　On them as they go rushing by;
They do not see their tearful eyes;
　They do not hear their plaintive sighs;
Their saddened looks no one discerns;
　O hardened hearts! God bless the bairns.

TO MY SISTER.

Dear sister mine, though far away,
   It matters not where'er I be,
Or whereso'er my footsteps stray,
   My fondest thoughts return to thee;
'Twas thee, when our dear mother died,
   Who watched o'er me with tender care,
And taught me sitting by thy side,
   To lisp the infant daily prayer.

Those early lessons taught by thee,
   I never, never, shall forget;
The truths you then instilled in me,
   Most fondly do I cherish yet;
And when temptations cross my way,
   And doubtful struggles rage within,
"My brother," then I hear you say,
   "Avoid the paths of vice and sin."

And then you take me as it were,
   As though I were a child again,
And lead me from the tempter's snare,
   And Satan's tempting is in vain;
And thus you ever follow me,
   No matter where my footsteps roam;
And thus I'm guided still by thee,
   As when a little boy at home.

O, shall I ever see thy face,
    My sister ever dear to me?
Or must I wait till death's embrace
    Shall set immortal spirit free?
If I could see thee but once more,
    Contentedly I then could wait,
Until we reached the golden shore,
    And entered through the pearly gate.

But when the thought I entertain,
    That life, at best, is but a span,
I think we'll never meet again,
    Upon this side of spirit-land.
My eyes then dim with sorrow's tear,
    And sadness overclouds my heart,
For none on earth to me so dear,
    My loving sister, as thou art.

But God, in whom my hopes remain,
    May yet my wand'ring footsteps guide,
And bring the wand'rer back again,
    In love and safety to thy side.
But if He wills we meet no more,
    Until our race on earth is run,
His holy name let us adore,
    And still repeat "Thy will be done."

I know thy earnest prayers ascend,
    That God may ever watch o'er me,
And still protect and me defend,
    And bring me safely back to thee;
But whether I return or not,
    In Him I trust and still rely;
And take sweet comfort from the thought,
    That I shall meet you By-and-bye.

REFLECTIONS.

Here in my room I sit alone,
　Beneath the shadows of the past;
Dear forms and faces long since gone,
　Appear as when I saw them last.

And here am I, a total wreck,
　Estranged from kindred and mankind;
I dread to let my thoughts turn back,
　Or take one single look behind.

My heart's a blank, my spirit's dead;
　I'm crushed and shattered from the strife;
Every spark of manhood's fled,
　And now I'm weary, sick of life.

O that memory was destroyed,
　That here, no longer it might reign;
For then I would not be annoyed,
　By thoughts that madly wreck my brain.

Why should it live and hold such sway,
　Recalling years forever gone?
From which in terror and dismay,
　I shrink, and dread to look upon.

Harrowing thoughts do still arise,
　From which, in vain, I try to flee;
And still those scenes come to my eyes,
　Which make this earth a hell to me.

And yet I know there was a time,
    But that's a long, long time ago,
When I was free from vice and crime,
    But now, alas, it is not so.

O, for those happy years, long fled,
    When I, in boyhood, used to play;
And night and morn would bow my head,
    To hear my darling mother pray.

But soon my path the tempter crossed,
    And I, in youth, was led astray;
My mother's prayers and tears were lost,
    The demon had me for his prey.

'Gainst all her prayers I steeled my heart,
    And all her counsels cast aside;
And when from her I would depart,
    Her pious teachings would deride.

At length she died, and I was left
    To battle through the world alone,
Of ev'ry kindred tie bereft,
    Without a friend to call my own.

Misguided by the worst of men,
    To vice and crime I fell a prey;
And for my acts committed then,
    Most sadly I repent to-day.

Wretch that I was, I took a wife,
    A lovely creature too was she,
Resolved to lead a better life,
    If such were possible for me.

My resolution was in vain;
  Instead of better I grew worse,
And shortly took to drink again,
  And this has been my greatest curse.

My wife with patience bore with me,
  Nor did she of her wrongs complain;
But begged and prayed most earnestly,
  That from the cup I would refrain.

To her entreaties I would bow,
  And turn aside to hide my tears;
And there most solemnly would vow,
  To change my course in future years.

Then she would kneel in earnest prayer,
  And ask the Lord to me sustain,
And guard me from the tempter's snare,
  And set my footsteps right again.

Then closer she would clasp our boy,
  And draw him to her loving breast;
And in her eyes a gleam of joy,
  Would shine like diamonds in a crest.

How soon, alas, was she to know,
  That all my vows were made in vain;
The tempter would not let me go,
  But held me fast in iron chain.

There is no hell, some people say,
  But them I caution to beware;
For thousands now are on the way,
  And Rum's the road that leads them there.

I gambled, drank, and reveled on,
　　The demon ever on my track,
Till hope and self respect were gone,
　　And I was left a total wreck.

My patient wife, heart broken now,
　　Became a victim of despair;
And soon upon her lovely brow,
　　Came marks of sorrow, grief, and care.

The brightness faded from her glance;
　　Her cheeks, once red, a paleness bore;
Her voice, that sounded sweetly once,
　　Contained its sweetness now no more.

Just as a rose that's left alone,
　　With neither heat nor rain supplied,
Will fade until its beauty's gone,
　　So she, neglected, drooped and died.

And for her death I am to blame;
　　To me her very life she gave;
'Twas me that brought her into shame,
　　And broken hearted to the grave.

As life was ebbing fast away,
　　On me a loving look she cast;
"Bend down," said she, "hear what I say,
　　I feel these words will be my last."

And as I knelt beside her bed,
　　Said she "a loving, dying wife,
Requests of you, when she is dead,
　　That you will lead a better life."

"To thee and Him who rules on high,
  I leave the only child I bore;
Now promise me before I die,
  That henceforth you will drink no more."

"But let me hear you promise this,
  And let me see my darling boy,
I'll seal your promise with a kiss,
  And leave the world on wings of joy."

Her ice cold hand in mine did rest,
  And looking on her face I swore,
That I would grant her last request,
  And henceforth I would drink no more.

A smile illumed her death pale face,
  "May heaven bless you here below;
And now let me my child embrace,
  And kiss you both before I go."

And thus her spirit passed away,
  Far, far, beyond this world of sin,
To realms of everlasting day,
  Where drunkards can not enter in.

Death came again in one decade,
  And snatched from me my darling boy;
And in the grave where he was laid,
  Was buried all my earthly joy.

Since then my life has been a load;
  And toward the grave I cheerless go,
Tottering on my weary road,
  Down burdened with remorse and woe.

But though of joy I am bereft,
  And life is but a burden now.
One consolation still is left,
  I have been faithful to my vow.

My sun of life will soon decline,
  For now I'm feeble, old, and gray;
And soon this fragile frame of mine,
  Will mingle with its kindred clay.

Relentless Death, for thee I wait,
  No terror in thy sting I see;
And yonder at the golden gate,
  Bright angels wait to welcome me.

FALLEN.

Now lost to my father and mother am I;
To brothers and sisters who now pass me by;
Now lost to the friends whom I dearly did love,
Now lost to myself and my Father above;
O hard was the heart that first led me astray,
From father, from mother, from virtue away,
Then left me forsaken, an object of scorn,
To deeply regret that I ever was born.

I never once thought I should have to endure,
The fate that now makes me so abject and poor,
Despised by my sex, to my name a disgrace,
Consenting to yield to man's sinful embrace.
An outcast from virtue, whose paths I have trod,
A mark of derision, forsaken of God,
Now brought to the depths of the bitterest woe,
And spurned and derided wherever I go.

The pangs of remorse sometimes reach to my heart,
And penitent tears all unbidden will start,
And though I'm an outcast estranged and alone,
My thoughts still revert to the years that are flown;
Oh, could I the steps I have taken retrace,
And leave this detested, most horrible place,
But such cannot be, I am lost to my all,
And I must endure the result of my fall.

People spurn me as vile, and treat me as such,
Consider me worthless, too loathsome to touch;
While he who first led me to ruin and shame,
Goes free from all censure, and free from all blame.
The end will soon come, and though outcast I be,
Perhaps there is One will take pity on me,
Who will to the injured his mercy extend,
And be to the outcast protector and friend.

"WINDOM."

A TRIBUTE.

The stillness of death filled the banquetting hall,
  And mantle of sadness the guests overspread,
A deep cloud of sorrow dropped over them all,
  As lowly 'twas whispered that Windom was dead.
Ah, little they thought, as they greeted with pride,
  The great financier, as he rose to the floor,
That shadow unseen had crept close to his side,
  And silently death had stole in at the door.

No more will his eloquence sound in the hall,
  Which people so greatly delighted to hear;
No more from his lips, like sweet music, will fall
  Brave words of encouragement, comfort and cheer.
His tongue now is silent, and hushed is his voice:
  His honored career has been brought to a close,
And he, who was wont to make others rejoice,
  Now sleeps in embrace of eternal repose.

As true as the needle that points to the pole,
  So Windom was true to his every trust;
His goodness of heart, and his greatness of soul,
  Prevented his being unkind or unjust.
A friend to the poor, who for succor would plead;
  His ear ever open to suffering's call;
His hand ever ready to help those in need;
  His face ever beaming with kindness for all.

In sadness, the head of the Nation is bowed,
   And gathering tears dim his sorrowful eye,
His soul is enveloped in grief like a shroud.
   A star has gone out from his beautiful sky.
Hereafter, in Cabinet Councils convened,
   The wisdom of Windom no longer will shine;
No longer will clouds, when they rise on the scene,
   Dissolve 'neath the light of his luminous mind.

And thee, Minnesota, in all coming years,
   Remember the glory and honor he won,
Bring garlands of flowers bedewed with thy tears,
   To place on the grave of thy true, noble son.
Though statues of bronze may be raised to his fame,
   And cold, silent marble his virtues may tell,
Yet shrines more enduring will rise to his name,
   In hearts of the people who loved him so well.

Windom, O! Windom, kind, noble, and true,
   The Nation now mourns thee, so faithful and brave,
The earth may enshroud thee, but tears shed for you,
   Like dew-drops from Heaven, will water thy grave;
Unlooked for, unthought of, yet sudden thy fall,
   Like soldier and hero, you died at your post;
The trumpet was sounded, you answered the call,
   And Heaven has gained what the Nation has lost.

May thine be the rest of the sanctified dead,
   And sweetly above thee may bright flowers bloom·
Still green be the sod that lies over thy head,
   And zephyrs from Heaven blow over thy tomb.
Though gone from us here to that beautiful land,
   Where love's shining banner is ever unfurled,
In bright golden letters forever will stand,
   The name that, untarnished, thou'st left to the world.

ALONE.

Alone I sit upon the shore,
　And gaze across the rolling sea,
And thoughts of what has long since passed,
　Come crowding to my memory.

Away upon the other shore,
　Far, far, across the deep blue waves,
My mother, and a brother too,
　Sleep there within their peaceful graves.

I see the house where I was born;
　The brook by which I often strayed;
The school house of my boyhood days;
　The fields and meadows where I played.

The little pond behind the hill,
　Where I in youth would often go,
To watch my tiny little boat
　As it went sailing to and fro.

The hazel wood where oft I've gone,
　With boys the ripened nuts to pull,
Or join in other sportive tricks,
　While praying truant from the school.

I see the grand old chestnut tree,
　To which I often would repair,
And tell the oft told tale of love
　To my sweet Mary sitting there.

O, for those happy, joyous days,
  To me that can return no more,
That I enjoyed in youthful years
  Upon yon foreign distant shore.

All, all, are now forever gone,
  Their pleasures and their joys are past,
And homeless here I sit alone,
  My heart with sorrow overcast.

No friend have I, to whom I might
  The cause of all my grief impart,
And though I had, he could not share
  The sad, sweet mem'ries of my heart.

The girl I loved, I made my wife
  Against my father's stern command,
And thus it is that now I roam
  A stranger in this distant land.

She, too, is dead and in her grave;
  Life's pathway now I tread alone,
And since my darling Mary died,
  My heart to joy has been unknown.

O, what is life embittered thus!
  Just like the doe when death is nigh,
With quiv'ring arrow in her breast,
  In search of quiet place to die.

Perhaps there is a brighter land,
  Beyond this vale of tears and pain,
Where weeping eyes and stricken hearts,
  May meet the lost and loved again.

A LOVER'S APPEAL.

I come once more ere I depart,
 To ask thy hand again;
O say not dearest of my heart,
 That now I plead in vain;
But could thine eye but enter here,
 Within this breast of mine,
There you would find a heart sincere,
 That is but only thine.

Can faithful love be bought and sold?
 Or do you cast aside
A loving heart, more dear than gold,
 To be a rich man's bride?
Do riches always blessings bring
 To those of wealth possessed?
How can the wounded warbler sing
 With arrow in its breast?

The rich may boast of acres wide,
 And mansions very grand;
Of ships that on the ocean ride,
 And wealth at their command;
No wealth have I on land or sea;
 No riches to impart;
And all that I can offer thee,
 Is true and loving heart.

These hands of mine, though rough they **be,**
 Can work for you and I;
And all that tends to comfort thee,
 With these I can supply;

And here's a true and faithful heart,
  That ever shall be thine,
Oh, say not, darling, we must part,
  But rather thou'lt be mine.

Reply.

Look at these sad and tear dimmed eyes,
  And read thine answer there;
Oh, would that it were otherwise,
  That I thy lot might share;
I vow before the God above,
  Here on my bended knee,
My tend'rest thoughts and warmest **love,**
  Shall ever be for thee.

Another must receive my hand,
  My heart is only thine,
A father's cruel, stern command,
  Forbids thee to be mine;
O God, thy blessing I invoke,
  And grant me strength I pray,
And though my life falls with the stroke,
  My father I obey.

O, blame me not, that it is so,
  That we are forced to part,
My greatest joy shall be to know,
  That thou hast still my heart;
My love, my love, thy pleading's vain,
  To father's will I bow;
We nevermore shall meet again;
  My heart is breaking now.

Adieu, one kiss before you go,
  To seal our mutual love,
And though we meet no more below,
  We'll meet again above;
And there we nevermore shall part,
  But with each other dwell,
And now beloved of my heart,
  A long and sad farewell.

SEQUEL.

The wedding bells proclaimed the day,
  When she the rich man wed;
But ere a month had passed away,
  The fair young bride was dead;
The tender flow'r so sweet and fair,
  Was crushed while yet in bloom;
A broken heart and sad despair
  Found her an early tomb.

Deprive the rose of light and heat,
  Its beauty soon is shed;
So loving hearts will cease to beat,
  When hope and joy have fled;
And thus she left a joyless home,
  For brighter one above,
And there she waits for him to come,
  To whom she gave her love.

GOOD-BYE, MOTHER DEAR.

I very soon must leave thee now,
   But do not weep, my mother dear;
Death's icy hand is on my brow,
   The parting time is drawing near;
Soon now will I be called to go,
   To leave this weary world of woe,
But we shall meet again, I know,
   To part no more, my mother dear.

I hear a voice I must obey,
   A voice that calls me, mother dear,
And now that I am called away,
   I cannot tarry longer here;
My sight grows dim, I cannot see,
   O, mother, still keep close by me,
For O, 'tis hard to part with thee,
   But part we must, my mother dear.

I feel a chill come o'er my heart,
   And I am cold, my mother dear;
From thee I now must soon depart,
   But do not shed a single tear;
O, do not weep when I am gone,
   We'll meet again around the throne,
One kiss before my spirit's flown,
   Then fare thee well, my mother dear.

Mother, it is hard to leave you,
    To suffer in this world of woe;
Do not let the parting grieve you,
    For we shall meet again, I know;
And ere I take my last good-bye,
    To dwell with angels up on high,
One tender kiss before I die,
    And then farewell, my mother dear.

TO A WOUNDED BIRD.

Ah, cruel, cruel, heartless man,
    Was not thy pity stirred,
When thou with most relentless hand,
    Didst wound this little bird?

Poor thing, thy voice is silent now,
    No more thy notes we'll hear,
No more thou'lt warble from the bough,
    To tell that spring is near.

No more thy song the morn will greet,
    To hail the new born day;
Nor fill the air with music sweet,
    By thy melodious lay.

O man, O man, what tempted thee,
    This act to perpetrate,
Didst not thine own humanity,
    Cry out to spare its fate?

Where was the voice of pity then,
  When this sad act occurred?
That thou must raise thy ruthless hand,
  To kill this little bird.

Is this the mercy thou wouldst have?
  Oh cruel, heartless man,
That e'en this little bird to save,
  Thou wouldst not stay thy hand.

Poor songster, how I pity thee,
  As wounded there you lie;
Hadst thou been beast to dreaded be,
  Then man from thee would fly.

Poor little thing, what couldst thou do,
  That thou shouldst murdered be;
That thou shouldst fall a victim to
  Man's heartless cruelty?

Relentless man, couldst thou not spare
  This harbinger of spring;
This feath'ry warbler of the air,
  Poor harmless little thing?

WILL WILLIE COME NO MORE?

Will Willie come no more, Ma-Ma?
   What makes him stay away?
I have no little brother now
   To go with me to play;
You know he called me to his side,
   And told me not to cry,
And said he had to leave me now,
   He'd meet me by-and-by.

And then, you know, he went to sleep
   Upon his little bed,
And you and Papa both did cry,
   And said that he was dead;
And Grandma, too, she cried, she did,
   And so did Uncle John,
And Auntie dressed him while he slept,
   And said, "poor Willie's gone."

And when I asked that Willie
   Might go with me to play,
You said that he was sleeping now,
   And could not go to-day;
And then I went to wake him up
   And kissed him on the cheek,
And did my little brother call,
   But Willie did not speak.

And then a little box was brought,
   And in this Willie lay,
Until one day some men came in
   And carried him away;
And now what makes you cry, Ma-Ma?
   Has Willie gone to stay?
And will he never come again
   To go with me to play?

My darling, Willie will not come,
   He's gone away to stay,
Your little brother nevermore
   Will go with you to play;
And though he is an angel now,
   I cannot help but cry,
But God will take us all, my dear,
   To meet him by-and-by.

'GENIE'S GRAVE.

Within a silent shady grove,
   The little darling's grave was made,
And there a mother's only child
   Most tenderly to rest was laid;
As tender flow'r while yet in bud,
   Is killed by cold and chilling frost,
So 'Genie in his childhood days,
   Was called to join the angel host.

The little warblers o'er his grave,
  Their cheerful notes will sweetly sing;
And from the earth that covers him,
  The brightest violets will spring;
And flowers sweet and roses fair,
  Around his grave will richly bloom,
And will their mingled perfume shed
  O'er little 'Genie's peaceful tomb.

When twilight shades begin to fall,
  And little birds have sought their nests,
A weeping mother may be seen
  Beside the spot where 'Genie rests;
And there, commingling with the dew,
  Her tears of grief and sorrow fall,
Upon the grave where sleeps her child,
  Her darling first-born and her all.

Weep not mother for your darling,
  An angel now he dwells on high;
Years roll on and time is fleeting,
  And you will meet him by-and-by;
Meet him where there's no more parting,
  Upon that bright and peaceful shore.
Where your darling waits your coming,
  To be united evermore.

A RAILROAD CATASTROPHE.

Thundering round the curvature,
  Sped on the flying train,
Hastening on like young gazelle
  That flies across the plain:
Flying onward through the darkness,
  Not knowing as it sped,
That such a sad catastrophe
  Awaited it ahead.

The night was dark, and onward dashed
  The fearless engineer,
No danger signal could he see
  And thought the track was clear,
But through the darkness as he peered,
  He saw to his dismay,
A light approaching rapidly,
  Off but a little way.

On went the brakes, the whistle blew,
  Still onward kept the train,
And shortly now the scene must change
  To one of death and pain:
The whistles screamed, the bells were rung
  On passenger and freight,
But still the trains kept speeding on
  To their impending fate.

The engineers leap from their posts,
  The trains together dash,
A cry of terror filled the air,
  As came the fearful crash;
Then mothers did their children clasp
  And husbands seized their wives,
And with the shock the trains upset
  With all their human lives.

Hear how the cries that call for help
  Ascend and rend the air;
Hear husbands, wives, and mothers
  Cry in grief and wild despair;
And hear the groans of mangled forms
  In agony and pain,
As helpless, bleeding, there they lie
  Beneath the shattered train.

See how the flames ascend on high,
  Oh, what a painful sight,
And from the fearful holocaust
  Comes wailing on the night;
Beyond the reach of human aid,
  They cry for help in vain,
And all unaided they must die
  Amid the burning train.

Father of mercy end the sight,
  So dreadful to behold;
The agony of such a scene
  By tongue can not be told;
The crackling timbers crumbling fall,
  The flames by wind are spread,
The victims' voices now are hushed
  And silent as the dead.

POLAND.

Afflicted land, by tyrants ruled,
　When will thy troubles cease?
When to thy homes will come again
　Security and peace?
When will thy people dare to speak,
　A word in humble praise,
Of thy brave sons who glory won,
　The Poles of former days?

Land of valiant Sobieski,
　Who fame and glory won,
In thee 'tis treason now to speak
　The name of thy brave son.
How long beneath the tyrant's yoke,
　Must thy brave people groan,
And wait to be restored again
　To freedom once their own?

Descendants of a noble race,
　Renowned in deeds of war,
How long must you endure the chains—
　The fetters of the Czar?
How long shall Cossack murderers—
　Mean slaves to royalty,
With iron heel and cruel rod,
　Reign masters over thee?

Ill fated land—once freedom's **home,**
　But now to bondage chained,
Where virgin purity is scoffed,
　And virtue is constrained;
Where but to love their native **land,**
　Is all that need be known,
To bring upon thy noble sons,
　The vengeance of a throne.

What land so curs'd by tyrants **rule?**
　What people so oppressed?
Thy wrongs awake deep sympathy,
　In ev'ry freeman's breast.
War clad assassins murder thee,
　Thy homes but prisons are,
On which espionage is kept,
　By minions of the Czar.

O, Poland, I could weep for thee;
　Thy wrongs stir up my soul;
In thee 'tis death or banishment,
　To say—"I am a Pole."
For loving thee, thy sons are doomed,
　The knout to undergo;
Or banished are to end their days,
　In wretchedness and woe.

Thy daughters too, subjected are
　To outrage, taunts, and sneers;
All unavailing are their prayers,
　Their pleadings and their tears;
In vain they utter their appeals,
　In vain for mercy call;
On ears to pity's voice unknown,
　Their implorations fall.

A Polish maid, named Kassowitz,
  Whose father had been slain,
Not long ago, within her home,
  Some friends did entertain;
And there conversing with her guests,
  Of danger unaware,
She spoke of Poland's wretchedness,
  And wrongs she had to bear.

The maid expressed her sympathy;
  Deplored her country's woes;
And mentioned how her father had
  Been murdered by his foes;
Bewailed the peoples' suffering,
  And hoped the day to see,
When God would strike the tyrants down,
  And set poor Poland free.

She little thought, among the guests
  Assembled at her board,
A Judas there had found a seat,
  Who marked her every word;
Who listened with attentive ear,
  To question and reply;
A viper paid by tyrant's gold,
  A Russian female spy.

At nine o'clock the guests dispersed,
  The time was drawing near,
When, by the laws imposed on Poles,
  All lights should disappear;
And now with crucifix in hand,
  The maiden kneels to pray,
But while she knelt rude Cossacks came,
  And carried her away.

Next morn a hollow square is **formed**;
  The Cossacks all turn out,
To see the maiden undergo
  The tortures of the knout;
Her tears are mocked, her pleading scoffed,
  And then with cruel haste,
Remorseless fiends seize hold of her,
  And strip her to the waist.

Bound hand and foot they tie her up,
  The lash is then applied;
Her flesh is torn, and blood runs down,
  Her wounded back and side;
No longer now she heeds the pain,
  Her sense of feeling's gone;
She swoons, she faints, but cannot fall,
  And still the knout's laid on.

Avenging God, in pity look,
  Upon this bleeding form;
And strike all tyrants from the earth,
  With thine uplifted arm.
Alas, alas, ye noble Poles,
  What wrongs are thine to tell;
No wonder freedom loudly shrieked,
  When "Kosciosko fell."

O God, avenge poor Poland's wrongs;
  Heal up her ev'ry scar;
And hurl Thy thunderbolts of wrath,
  Against the cruel Czar.
And speed the day, O God. I pray,
  When all the world shall see,
Oppression buried in the dust,
  And Poland once more free.

MILL CREEK VALLEY.

WAUBAUNSEE COUNTY, KAS.

Alone I sit on Buff'lo mound,
　The highest point for miles around,
And in the valley down below,
　I see the creek in riplets flow.
As I attempt its course to trace,
　I sometimes lose its shining face,
But lucent, sparkling, bright and clear,
　Still farther on it does appear.
I see it turn the distant bend,
　As towards the Kaw it doth descend,
And in the distance, far ahead,
　It looks just like a silver thread.

Like burnished steel its surface lies,
　Beneath the bright and azure skies,
But ever gliding towards the sea,
　In graceful sinuosity.
At times it glitters 'neath the rays
　Of summer sun, that with it plays;
Again it takes a sombre hue,
　As shaded by the oak and yew;
But as it nears the Kaw's embrace,
　Its farther course I fail to trace,
Then turn my gaze on scenes more fair,
　Than Burns e'er saw on banks of Ayr.

Before me, stretched across the plain,
  Lie waving fields of yellow grain,
And pleasant homes, where folk abide
  Whose ev'ry want is well supplied,
While blooming wild flow'rs, rich and rare,
  With sweetest perfume fill the air.
Scattered in groups, o'er pastures green,
  The browsing cattle may be seen,
And far as vision can be borne,
  Extend great fields of tasselled corn,
All blending in a grander sight,
  Than Moses saw from Pisgah's height.

Those steeples pointing towards the sky,
  Tell that is where St. Mary's lie;
And yonder, where that smoke expands,
  Is where Topeka proudly stands,
And in the intervening space,
  Woods, hills, and valleys interlace,
And leafy groves, on ev'ry hand,
  Their shadows throw across the land,
While cow-bells jingling from the brink,
  Tell where the cattle go to drink,
All constituting scene so grand,
  It seems like some enchanted land.

A long way off, beyond the bend,
  I see the engine smoke ascend,
And, curling up above the trees,
  Is scattered by the floating breeze,
And soon, like diamond drops of dew,
  Dissolves and passes out of view.
A rumbling sound comes to my ear,
  Like distant ocean drawing near,

And soon, appearing on the plain,
  Comes on the west-bound flying train,
And on it speeds like frightened doe,
  Across the valley down below.

Up from the woods that skirt the creek,
  The feath'ry warblers sweetly speak;
The red-bird, linnet, cushat-dove,
  All sing their sweetest songs of love,
And from the thicket, 'neath the hill,
  Comes up the cry of whip-poor-will.
I gaze enraptured on the scene,
  And ask, what Eden must have been;
If it more lovely was than this,
  It surely was a place of bliss,
For here sits beauty unexcelled,
  Unequaled, and unparalleled.

O, charming spot! Most lavishly
  Hath mother Nature dealt by thee,
For who, beneath bright heaven's dome,
  Could wish for more delightful home?
The bard might sit here day by day,
  And sweetly sing his life away.
Who can the argument advance,
  Such loveliness all sprung from Chance?
Who on such scenes can cast his eye,
  And then the living God deny?
O Thou who wast, and still shalt be,
  All Life and Beauty come from Thee.

TO JOSEPHINE.

Farewell, my darling Josephine,
  The time has come when we must part;
That I must go and leave thee now,
  With sadness overclouds my heart.

But when from thee I'm far away,
  I'll think how happy I have been,
In other days when by the side
  Of thee, my charming Josephine.

But better it would be for me,
  Could I forget I'd ever seen
A face so lovely and so fair
  As that of winsome Josephine.

The prize I sought I cannot reach,
  Too great the gulf that lies between,
Still on my heart shall be impressed
  The image of fair Josephine.

Dare I but hope; but no, alas;
  There is no hope on which to lean,
For now I see, when 'tis too late,
  That lost to me is Josephine.

And now farewell; when I am gone,
  And seas are rolling us between,
One passing thought is all I ask
  From thee, sweet, charming Josephine.

INFIDELITY REBUKED.

Begone, begone, speak not to me,
  From thy deceitful heart;
I've learned to know thy treachery,
  Get hence, I say, depart.
Go, worship at another shrine
  The image you adore,
For that deceitful heart of thine
  Is sought by me no more.

Ah, cruel wretch, go, quit my sight,
  You've turned that heart to stone;
That loved thee with such fond delight,
  And beat for thee alone;
Go, seek the one so highly born,
  So dearly prized by thee;
Her fingers with these rings adorn,
  That once you gave to me.

No grief within my heart shall swell,
  No pangs shall rend my breast.
Go, seek the one you love so well,
  Thy presence I detest;
And nevermore to me return
  Thy pledges to restore:
Thy heart is false, thy hand I spurn,
  Begone, sir, there's the door.

KISS ME DARLING AND YOU'LL SEE.

SHE.

Do not touch me gay deceiver,
　　False and fickle that thou art;
Seek the one you love so dearly,
　　Take thy presence hence—depart.

HE.

What's the matter with thee darling?
　　Why so rude and cold to me?
If you think I love another,
　　Kiss me darling and you'll see.

SHE.

Could I only but believe thee,
　　But that I fear I cannot do;
I that loved thee, Oh, so dearly,
　　To be cast off and spurned by you.

HE.

Why continue thus thy taunting?
　　Why think I will not faithful be?
If you think I'm false and fickle,
　　Kiss me darling and you'll see.

SHE.

Leave me, leave me, cease thy tempting,
　　Gay deceiver that thou art;
Once thy words I cherished fondly,
　　But now they lacerate my heart.

HE.

Now my darling well thou knowest,
   None else I ever loved but thee;
If you think that I am faithless,
   Kiss me darling and you'll see.

SHE.

Dare I trust thee, I would fondly
   Embrace thee in my arms again;
But to think how I have loved thee,
   Now makes my heart pulsate with pain.

HE.

Hush, my darling, hush I pray thee,
   Speak not such cruel words to me;
If you think I am not faithful,
   Kiss me darling and you'll see.

SHE.

I believe thee, I believe thee,
   Dearest, truest, come to me;
Nevermore my tongue shall chide thee,
   About thy infidelity.

HE.

Happy, happy, blissful ending,

SHE.

As lovers' quarrels should ever be,

HE.

No more taunting, no more chiding,

SHE.

Kiss me darling and you'll see.

MARY.

Enchanting is Mary,
Both winsome and airy,
I would give all the world to possess her,
And her heart I am sure,
Is both gentle and pure,
She's a sweet little creature, God bless her.

She is charming and gay
As the flowers of May,
And may no earthly sorrow distress her;
May grief never arise
To bring tears to her eyes,
She's a sweet little creature, God bless her.

She is fair as a rose,
That in midsummer grows,
'Twould be pleasure untold to caress her,
Were she only my wife,
I'd be happy for life,
She's a sweet little creature, God bless her.

She's a model of grace,
With a heavenly face,
How I wish I knew how to impress her;
Her bright smiles fascinate,
And her ways captivate,
She's a sweet little creature, God bless her.

As the stars in the night,
Her eyes sparkle as bright,
And her glance would enchant a professor;
Not a lilly so fair,
That with her can compare,
She's a sweet little creature, God bless **her.**

As snow she is chaste,
With a neat, slender waist,
And of beauty angelic possessor;
Never music so choice,
As the sound of her voice,
She's a sweet little creature, God bless **her.**

She is bright as the sun,
And my heart she has won,
As a suitor I now will address her,
She may answer me—nay,
But be that as it may,
She's a sweet little creature, God bless her.

TO A YOUNG LADY.

My wrinkled brow and silvered hair,
　Bespeak my years as not a few;
I've tasted pleasures rich and rare,
　And deeply drank of sorrow too.
Full well I know, and am aware,
　That hope the youthful heart will cheer;
I, too, built "castles in the air;"
　Like mist I saw them disappear.

That time of life for me is o'er,
   And down the hill I'm going fast;
I've sailed the sea from shore to shore,
   And soon my anchor will be cast.
To you life's sea seems calm and clear,
   And thus, I trust, 'twill ever be,
But treach'rous breakers may be near,
   Although, just now, unseen by thee.

Emotions shortly thou may'st know,
   As yet unfelt by thee, I trow,
And trials thou may'st undergo,
   Of which you little dream of now.
Guard well thy heart 'gainst suitors' wiles,
   However earnest they appear;
Be not too lavish with thy smiles,
   Nor take for granted all you hear.

The world to thee is yet unknown,
   Its thorny paths thou may'st not see;
But round thee meshes may be thrown,
   And snares be set to capture thee.
You do not know what dangers lie,
   Like hidden rocks, along the way;
Or how some vip'rous wretch may try,
   To lead thy youthful steps astray.

Learn this, before it is too late,
   'Tis not the honeyed speech that's true;
For often men dissimulate,
   To hide what they intend to do.
'Tis not the brainless jackanape,
   So perfumed and so dandified,
Nor yet the college-cultured ape,
   That e'er should win thee for a bride.

The rustic swain that tills the soil,
    Unschooled in manners though he be,
Who earns his bread by daily toil,
    May have a heart that's worthy thee.
Is not the sweetest scented rose
    Supported by a thorny stem?
The roughest casket may disclose
    The richest, choicest, brightest gem.

Should Cupid strike you with his dart,
    To make it known be not too free,
But lock the secret in your heart,
    And safely then conceal the key.
By flatterers be not deceived,
    However sweet their words may fall,
For very oft their sweetest speech
    Is only bitterness and gall.

'Tis hard to conquer love I know;
    But better drown it out in tears,
Than suffer wretchedness and woe,
    And bitterness in after years.
Bear this in mind, for 'tis a truth,
    That love as pure as ever borne,
Is oft misplaced by trusting youth,
    On those who pay it back with scorn.

Now, Dora, I have counseled thee,
    As though thou wert a child of mine,
And do not deem it rude of me
    Or take a single word unkind.
No other wish have I for thee,
    Than that of aged, dearest friend,
Whose lengthened life must shortly be,
    Like this my counsel, at an end.

I WANT TO KISS PAPA ONCE MORE.

Prepared for the grave in his coffin he lay,
    And mourners stood weeping, surrounding the bier;
They gazed on his form, now inanimate clay,
    With sorrowful hearts, and fast falling tear;
But weeping and wailing disturbed not the sleep,
    Of him whom the mantle of death was spread o'er;
But Oh, it was sad to behold his child weep,
    And hear how she plead, to kiss papa once more.

How touchingly sad was the child in her woe,
    As burdened with sorrow she bowed her young head;
How cold all the comfort that words could bestow,
    As weeping she looked on the face of the dead;
Poor, sad stricken heart, now to sorrow allied,
    The Savior alone can thy comfort restore;
Look up to the cross, where the Comforter died,
    And papa will kiss his loved darling once more.

The funeral march, so impressive to hear,   [strains;
    Was performed by the band in slow measured
Tow'rds the city of rest the cortege drew near,
    To lay in the tomb a dear brother's remains;
The line moved in silence, but many an eye
    By gathering tear long unmoistened before,
Grew dim as the child in her sorrow would cry,
    "Oh, let me kiss papa, dear papa, once more."

The grave was prepared, and 'mid silence profound,
  The coffin was lowered within the dark cell;
Save the chant of the dirge, was heard not a sound,
  As over the casket bright evergreens fell;
And thus a dear brother was laid to his rest;
  The funeral rites of the Order were o'er;
But still could be heard the child's plaintive request,
  To let her kiss papa, dear papa, once more.

'Midst sad stricken hearts, in my time I have been,
  Where keen darts of sorrow have entered my breast;
But never before, at the sad sights I've seen,
  Have I been so deeply and sadly impressed;
Where battle raged fiercely, 'midst slaughter I've stood,
  And comrade's I've seen stricken down by the score;
But these I beheld in less sorrowful mood,
  Than when the child cried to kiss papa once more.

CHRISTMAS MORNING.

All hearts should this morning be joyful and glad,
  And yet mine is heavy, despondent and sad;
For well do I know, in the gifts he bestowed,
  That Santa Claus slighted our humble abode.

Soon boys, with their drums, will be rattling away,
  And beautiful dolls, little girls will display;
A few will have wagons, and some be supplied
  With nice wooden horses to mount on and ride.

What wonderful presents old Santa Claus brings;
  What boxes of candy, and beautiful things;
Nice guns to play soldier, and trumpets to blow,
  Are all brought by Santa from regions of snow.

Tin rattles for babies; and numberless toys
  In order he placed, for the girls and the boys;
But Santa neglected to give us a call,
  And my little darlings got nothing at all.

I soon heard the sound of their pattering feet;
  I heard their young voices the Lord's prayer repeat;
Then down stairs they scampered with hearts full of glee,
  All shouting at once, "Merry Christmas" to me.

I kissed each one fondly, 'twas all I could do,
  And sadly replied, "Merry Christmas to you;"
My eyes filled with tears that I could not suppress,
  And prayed God devoutly my children to bless.

They looked round the room, and their tears could be
      traced,
  For stockings hung empty just where they were
      placed;
Then sweet little Bessie, to me she did come,
    And "Papa," said she, "Santa Taus didn't tum."

I gathered them round me, and to them I read
  Of Him by whose bounty the ravens are fed;
And told them of One whose kind love would endure,
  Who blessed them and loved them, although they
      were poor.

I looked at them all and distinctly could see,
  A much greater comfort than riches to me;
A something I valued much higher than wealth,
  And offered up thanks for the blessing of health.

ON SEEING A YOUNG MAN
INSTANTLY KILLED.

How truthfully it has been said,
    The fleeting life of man,
No longer is at any time,
    Than but a single span.

This hour we see him full of life,
    Not thinking what's before;
But like a flash, death comes along,
    The next he is no more.

To-day he's hopeful, cheerful, strong,
    Life's future seems so clear;
A thought he does not entertain,
    That death is standing near.

Oh, what a deep and solemn thought,
    For mortal man to have,
To think to-day he's full of life,
    To-morrow in the grave.

In health and strength, in mirth and joy,
    Remember this, O man,
That death may take you unprepared,
    And life is but a span.

DROWNED.

Drowned. Oh, my God! My only son!
  Drowned, did you say! O, where!
Merciful God, this fearful stroke
  Is more than I can bear.

Did you say drowned? It cannot be,
  It is not so, I know;
My darling, much-loved only son,
  Ah, tell me 'tis not so.

My heart will break. Was no one near
  My darling boy to save!
Oh, can it be, that now he sleeps
  Within a wat'ry grave?

My God, for what am I reserved!
  Lying in the river;
My son, my hope, my joy, my life,
  Lost to me forever.

Can it be so? Ah, surely no,
  The only child I had;
Oh, tell me that he is not drowned,
  The thought will drive me mad.

Drowned, my boy! No, no, he lives,
  I see him standing there;
Look how the water's dripping from
  His dark and glossy hair.

He's gone.   So soon.   My boy, come back.
  Why leave your mother sad!
He will not come.   He's drowned, he's drowned;
  Oh God, I'm surely mad.

My boy, my boy, your mother comes,
  She shortly will be there;
Help, help, O help my son to save,
  Have pity on despair.

What feeling's this comes over me,
  That chills me through and through?
Oh welcome messenger of death;
  My boy I come to you.

THANKSGIVING.

Though fully aware that my blessings are few;
Though I'm far from my home and penniless too;
Though somewhat despondent and cheerless I be,
That things are no worse I am thankful to Thee.

Though empty my purse, and uncertain my fare,
I envy not those who have much and to spare;
For well I remember when I, with the rest,
Was numbered with those so abundantly blessed.

Yet I make no complaint, for mine is the blame,
And God, in his goodness, continues the same;
Though heavy the burden that on me is cast,
I render Him thanks for his gifts in the past.

Let those who to-day on the choicest may dine,
Return earnest thanks to the giver Divine,
And though I have nothing, still thankful I'll be,
That others are blessed, though no blessing for me.

No matter what burdens we have to endure,
Or whether we're rich or distressedly poor;
We all can be thankful for what has been done,
And render Him thanks for the gift of his **Son.**

THE BROKEN PLIGHT.

Now the plight of love is broken,
  Made long ago 'tween you and me;
And your false, deceitful token,
  With scorn I now return to thee.

I prized it once, but now I spurn
  The gift of one whom truth denies,
Yet not the ring that I return.
  But he that gave it I despise.

No wish have I to still retain
  A token of thy faithless vow,
Nor do I wish to see again
  The face by me detested now.

Who would have thought that one so fair
  Was nothing but a flatt'ring cheat,
And that the smiles he used to wear,
  Could cover up such base deceit.

How could I know that in your breast,
  A pois'nous reptile nestled there,
While I so fondly you caressed
  And vowed none else thy love should share.

But now the serpent shows its fangs,
  And shoots at me its poisoned dart,
And though its sting may cause some pangs,
  It shall not hurt or wound my heart.

That one fond thought I gave to thee,
  Brings to my cheek a blush of shame,
But hateful now thou art to me,
  And I abhor thy very name.

Think not the parting I regret,
  Or that from me one tear shall fall,
For by to-morrow I'll forget
  That such a wretch doth live at all.

Don't think my cup is filled with gall,
  Or that for thee I'll sigh and weep;
For I assure thee once for all,
  I shall not lose one moment's sleep.

TO HARRY

Since Maud loves another, in thee it is vain
  To cherish the hope that her heart you can gain,
But this is no reason you reckless should be,
  For good fish in plenty are still in the sea.

Why trouble your mind about things that can't be?
  'Tis plain that her love's not intended for thee;
Then why should you languish, and comfort refuse,
  Because some one else has stepped into your shoes?

You looked upon Maud as an angel divine;
  But since you can't have her, why need you repine?
For nectar as sweet may be yet thine to sip,
  As ever you drank from the fount of her lip.

Just give her your blessing and let her depart,
  And banish her out of your mind and your heart;
Once more cast your net in the trough of the sea,
  And fish just as good may come floating to thee.

Bear in mind that our good, kind grandmother Eve,
  Our first parent Adam did basely deceive;
And woman's deception, thus early began,
  Caused the sin of the world, and ruin of man.

Delilah did Samson most foully betray,
  And unto the Phillistines gave him away;
Though thousands he slew, with donkey's jaw-bone,
  By woman's deceit he was conquered alone.

Not all are deception, there's one that I know,
　As pure as an angel, as spotless as snow;
As true to her lover as needle to pole,
　Her kiss is the joy and delight of my soul.

You think, peradventure, that Maud is to blame;
　But why did you leave until sure of your game?
And while you may think she's a cheat and a fraud,
　There are worse in the world than sweet little Maud.

And now to conclude, just permit me to say,
　Take things as they come, let them come as they may;
Still bearing in mind when you make your complaints,
　That masculine sinners outnumber the saints.

DEPARTED AUTUMN.

Gentle Autumn has departed,
　And now cold winter is at hand;
The trees have shed their summer leaves
　And now in nakedness they stand.

The howling wind most fiercely blows,
　And bears a dismal doleful sound,
The drifting snow drives madly on
　Across the hardened, frozen ground.

Without, 'tis gloomy, dark, and drear,
　And cheerless too the scene within;
The only sound that greets the ear,
　Comes from the raging howling wind.

The sky above is overcast,
 The clouds hang heavy, thick, and low;
And mother earth, with features veiled,
 Enshrouded lies beneath the snow.

Yes, Autumn's gone, and Summer too,
 The feathered songsters all have fled;
And fragrant flowers, withered now,
 Their sweet perfumes no longer shed.

And as the seasons, so is man
 To many changes subject here,
'Tis summer now, he's in his bloom,
 But soon the bloom will disappear.

Life's winter's creeping slowly on,
 And soon will come the blighting blast,
When man, like flowers too must fade,
 And wither, droop, and die at last.

Now comes the thought, the solemn thought,
 Beyond man's knowledge to explain;
When we have died and passed away,
 Shall we, like flowers, bloom again?

DEAD AND UNKNOWN.

(In 1879, a young English officer, who went to the West on a hunting tour, was found dead on the plains. His trappings bore the name of *Bainbridge*.)

A stranger in a foreign land,
    He died upon the plain;
No loved one there to take his hand,
    Or cool his fevered brain.
Far, far from home and friends most dear,
    Uncared for and alone,
The stranger died, and not a tear
    Was shed for the unknown.

But there are eyes that tears shall dim
    Upon Old England's shore,
And there are hearts shall bleed for him,
    To learn he is no more.
An aged father waiting there,
    Shall grieve for him that's gone;
A weeping mother in despair
    Shall mourn her noble son.

A sister, too, in sad distress,
    Shall tears of sorrow shed,
And wring her hands in bitterness
    To learn her brother's dead.
And one may be whose heart shall swell
    With grief and throbbing pain,
To learn that him she loved so well,
    Died friendless on the plain.

There is a wound no balm can heal;
   There is a sootheless grief;
A pain that stricken hearts must feel,
   Till death affords relief.
Yes, hearts shall mourn, and eyes shall weep,
   For him who died unknown,
And went to his eternal sleep
   Uncared for and alone.

AMONG THE DEAD.

Here sleep the dead in peaceful rest,
   From ev'ry earthly trouble free;
And here I stand with grief oppressed,
   And wish the grave did cover me.

O hallowed rest, O sweet repose,
   With aching heart I wait the day,
When death my weary eyes shall close,
   And I am laid beneath the clay.

By grief is seared my youthful brow,
   My load is great, too great to bear;
O that I slept as ye do now,
   Free from trouble, grief and care.

Within a churchyard far away,
   The greatest joy to me e'er known,
Now sleeps in death beneath the clay,
   While here I stand alone, alone.

The ivy now surrounds the tomb,
  Of her whose loss I much deplore;
Upon her grave the roses bloom,
  But she who sleeps will wake no more.

Her angel face now smiles on me,
  As here among the dead I stand;
O that my spirit too might flee
  To that delightful spirit land.

Soon, soon, departed I'll be there;
  This fragile barque no pow'r can save;
For wrecked by sorrow, grief and care,
  It soon must sink into the grave.

Sleep on, sleep on, ye silent dead,
  Thy lot is one we all must share;
When all we loved on earth hath fled,
  Life's then a burden hard to bear.

But short's the time we have to stay,
  For life is but a fleeting breath;
And men, like flowers, soon decay,
  The closing scene of all is death.

DRIFTING.

Down the stream of Time we're drifting,
  Like chips upon the river breast,
Tossed and tumbled by the eddy,
  And never finding place to rest.
Drifting on we know not whither,
  Like feathers floating in the air;
Driven by each changing current,
  But drifting still, we know not where.

Now we float in placid waters,
  And calm and peacefully we go;
Now we're lashed by raging billows,
  Now plunged into the gulf below.
Thus forever we are drifting,
  As chips drift onward toward the sea,
Ever restless, ever moving
  Toward the vast eternity.

Floating corks upon life's ocean,
  We drift along upon the wave,
Hoping, doubting, trusting, fearing,
  Still drifting nearer to the grave.
Mere puppets of a fleeting hour,
  We scud before the flying gale,
Human wrecks are all around us,
  But yet we never shorten sail.

Before us breakers may be lying,
   And hurricanes may fiercely blow,
Storms may drive us far to leeward,
   As down the stream of Time we go.
We have left the Past behind us,
   And, O, how swift the moments flee,
Now we're drifting through the Present,
   Beyond which all is mystery.

One and all, we are but floaters
   Down the current of the stream,
And when the bound'ry we have passed,
   We'll be as some forgotten dream.
Calms may lengthen out our journey,
   And storms may drive us close to shoal,
Still we drift forever onward,
   Approaching nearer to the goal.

And now at last the goal is reached,
   The anchor's dropped and we are free;
We've floated down the stream of Time,
   To realms of sweet Nonentity.
The drifting now is at an end,
   And back we go to Mother earth,
Whose loving breast had nurtured us
   Since first our being had its birth.

I MISS MY BAIRNS.

I miss my bairns, I miss my bairns,
    An' richt sair is my heart;
I did'na think how hard 'twad be,
    When frae them I did part;
I canna see them romp an' play,
    Which aye my heart did cheer;
I canna see their dimpled smiles,
    To me sae sweet an' dear.

I canna see them rin a race,
    A' laughin' as they came,
To see which o' them wad be first
    To meet me comin' hame;
Nae doot their wee bit childish hearts,
    Are sair as weel's my ain,
An' tears rin doon their little cheeks,
    To think they're left alane.

But by their mither as they kneel
    Each morn an' nicht, I ken,
As they repeat their simple prayers,
    They think o' papa then;
But sair I miss their guid nicht kiss,
    Which they were wont to gie;
An' when I think o' them, puir bairns,
    My tears I canna stay.

But to His care, wha bairnies love,
    The God in whom I trust,
I leave them, fully satisfied
    That He is guid an' just;
To them a father He will be,
    Nae odds what may befa',
An' this it is that comforts me,
    Whilst frae them I'm awa.

PERISHED IN THE SNOW.

Two little children hand in hand,
    Set out for school one wintry day,
The snow was falling thick and fast,
    In which the children lost the way.
The bell was rung, the roll was called,
    To "Willie Stewart" no answer came,
Nor did there any voice respond,
    At call of little Eva's name.

The absent children wandered on,
    Not knowing they had gone astray,
And Eva to her brother said,
    "Willie, the school seems far away."
"We'll soon be there," the boy replied,
    "We must have come a mile or more,
Although the distance seems to be
    Much farther than it was before."

Each step the little wand'rers took,
 But led them farther from the way,
And crying, little Eva said,
 "Willie, we won't reach school to-day."
The boy peered through the falling snow,
 Still thinking that the school was near,
But to his eager little eyes,
 The looked for house did not appear.

And when the hour for recess came,
 Their little schoolmates scamp'ring go,
To play their childish, mirthful games,
 While they were wand'ring through the snow
The school's dismissed, then homeward go
 The scholars in a straggling train,
But there are two whose little feet,
 Will never bring them home again.

Poor little hearts, alone and lost,
 And none their feeble cry to hear,
For now they wander through the woods,
 Lost in the snow and night is near.
"Willie, my feet are growing sore,"
 His sister to him did remark,
"I'm very cold, and hungry too,
 And, Willie, it is getting dark."

"My little sister, we are lost,"
 And Willie's tears began to flow,
"But papa will come after us
 And take us home with him I know."
"O, Willie, I am very weak,
 And papa may not come I fear,
You go and tell him to make haste,
 And till you come I'll tarry here."

"I cannot leave you," Willie said,
  "To stay here in the woods alone,
Besides my little sister dear,
  The way to go to me's unknown;
Here I will stay along with thee,
  For see how dark it has become,
And then when papa comes for us,
  He'll find us both and take us home.'

Then little Eva, crying, said,
  "I cannot any farther go,
Let us sit down and wait for Pa,
  Beside this tree, upon the snow."
Then Willie spread his overcoat,
  And round his sister's neck he tied
The scarf he wore, and then sat down
  With little Eva by his side.

Benumbed and famished, cold and weak,
  They sat and wept, O painful sight;
"Wille," and faintly Eva spoke,
  "Papa will not be here to-night."
"Willie, I want to sleep, don't you?
  Let us our prayers to God repeat,
Just as we do each night at home,
  While kneeling at dear Mamma's feet.

The prayers were said, the children slept,
  Cheek pressed to cheek and side by side,
And locked within each other's arms,
  Little brother and sister died.
And while they slept bright angels came,
  And set their little spirits free,
And soared with them to Him who said,
  "Let little children come to me."

To trace the little wand'ring feet,
  Men searched the country all around,
And though continued all night long,
  The missing children were not found.
Next morning came; the search went on,
  Nor were they found till late that day,
Dead in each other's fond embrace,
  From home full fifteen miles away.

O, what a picture 'twas to see!
  So painful, yet extremely fair.
Face turned to face, asleep in death,
  They found the little wand'rers there.
What tongue can tell the father's grief?
  What pen portray the mother's woe?
And strong men wept to hear the tale
  Of how they perished in the snow.

(The sad incident upon which the foregoing poem is founded,
occurred in Boonton, New Jersey, several years ago.)

AN INVOCATION.

Most merciful Father, Thy spirit bestow,
  To comfort and cheer me wherever I go;
To lead me, to guide me, be Thou ever near,
  To guard and protect me whilst tarrying here.

Deep into my heart let Thy spirit descend,
  And be Thou to me a protector and friend,
And lift up my soul from the depths of its sin,
  That Thy holy spirit may enter therein.

O, teach me to love Thee, Thy name to adore,
  And teach me to walk in Thy ways evermore,
And teach me to live, that when death comes to me.
  'Twill be but the portal that leads me to Thee.

And grant, dearest Father, when life's troubles cease,
  My soul may find rest in Thy mansions of peace,
There dwell undisturbed, free from sorrow and pain,
  Redeemed and made pure by the Lamb that was
    slain.

TRUST HIM.

There is One who is your friend,
  Trust Him;
He'll be faithful to the end,
  Trust Him;
Should you sail misfortune's sea,
Lashed by want and poverty,
He will be a friend to thee;
  Trust Him.

Should you faint upon the way,
  Trust Him;
Should all others you betray,
  Trust Him;
If on Him you but depend.
You will always find a friend,
True and faithful to the end;
  Trust Him.

Should temptations you assail,
 Trust Him;
Should your faith begin to fail,
 Trust Him;
Thy strength He will renew,
And will safely guide you through,
And sustain and strengthen you;
 Trust Him.

When by trouble sorely pressed,
 Trust Him;
If by sorrow you're distressed,
 Trust Him;
You will ever find Him near,
With attentive, willing ear,
All thy sad complaints to hear;
 Trust Him.

If afflictions you must bear,
 Trust Him;
When burdened down with care,
 Trust Him;
He'll remove thy burdens quite,
And thy footsteps guide aright,
He will lead thee to the light;
 Trust Him.

Should trials overtake you,
 Trust Him;
Should other friends forsake you,
 Trust Him;
You will find Him ever true,
Kind and sympathetic too,
He will aid and succor you;
 Trust Him.

When the head is bowed in grief,
 Trust Him;
When the heart sighs for relief,
 Trust Him;
At the door He's waiting there,
And most gladly He will share,
All the griefs you have to bear;
 Trust Him.

When great waves of trouble roll,
 Trust Him;
When deep anguish rends the soul,
 Trust Him;
When clouds of dark despair
Gather round you ev'rywhere,
Seek Him earnestly in prayer;
 Trust Him.

When by fate you're roughly tossed,
 Trust Him;
When all hope to you seems lost,
 Trust Him;
When old friends do you deny,
And in coldness pass you by,
Upon Him you can rely;
 Trust Him.

When sad and weary-hearted,
 Trust Him;
When fondest ties are parted,
 Trust Him;
Then His loving voice you'll hear,
Speaking words of hope and cheer,
And he'll wipe away the tear;
 Trust Him.

When deserted and alone,
 Trust Him;
If rejected by your own,
 Trust Him;
He will all thy wrongs redress,
And will lighten thy distress,
He will comfort thee and bless;
 Trust Him.

When the heart in sorrow sighs,
 Trust Him;
When some loved and dear one dies,
 Trust Him;
He'll remove the painful dart,
From the wounded bleeding heart,
And sweet healing will impart;
 Trust Him.

When cold death comes on at last,
 Trust Him;
When your sight is dimming fast,
 Trust Him;
Then bright visions you will see,
As you near eternity,
Of the home prepared for thee;
 Trust Him.

As you close your eyes in death,
 Trust Him;
As you draw your parting breath,
 Trust Him;
Then thy soul will take its flight,
To the land of pure delight,
There with loved ones to unite,
 Trust Him.

WHY WILL YOU DIE?

O, thoughtless man, why still pursue
    The paths that lead to death and sin?
Yonder is a fold of glory,
    And Christ invites you to walk in.

Why go down to endless ruin?
    Forget'st thou hast a soul to save?
Hast no hope of future glory,
    Beyond the dark and dismal grave?

O, sinner, turn, why should you die?
    Why not return to God and live?
No matter what thy sins may be,
    Return to God, he will forgive.

He takes no pleasure in thy death,
    Then why the paths of death pursue?
Did He not give, that thou might'st live,
    His only Son to die for you?

Behold Him nailed upon the cross,
    Behold His pierced and bleeding side,
And all for you He suffered this,
    For you the Son was crucified.

Behold the man unknown to guile,
    Extended on the bloody tree;
Behold His temples crowned with thorns,
    And all, poor sinner, all for thee.

For you the spotless Lamb was slain,
    To purify you of your sin,
And at your heart He's knocking now,
    And pleading strongly to get in.

Must all His pleading be in vain?
    Wilt thou not let the Savior in?
Thy wand'ring steps He'll guide aright,
    And lead you from the paths of sin.

GET THE PASSWORD.

Have you got the password, brother,
    Can you enter at the gate?
If you have not, get it quickly,
    By-and-by may be too late;
Time is fleeting, life's uncertain,
    And your moments may be few;
If you cannot give the password,
    No admission is for you.
         Get the password, get the password,
            There is danger in delay;
         Hasten quickly, find the Master,
            He will tell thee what to say.

Only brothers true and tested
    Enter in without delay;
Those who have not got the password,
    Shall be promptly turned away;

Implorations will not aid thee,
  And thy tears will useless be;
If thy cross thou wilt not carry,
  There shall be no Crown for thee.
        Get the password, get the password,
          There is danger in delay;
        Hasten quickly, find the Master,
          He will tell thee what to say.

At the door the Guardian's standing,
  Waiting for the word from you;
If you cannot give the password,
  You can never enter through;
Haste my brother, get the password,
  Closed the wicket soon may be;
If you tarry, you may find it
  Closed for all eternity.
        Get the password, get the password, .
          There is danger in delay;
        Hasten quickly, find the Master,
          He will tell thee what to say.

Get the password, get the password,
  Time is fleet as the wind;
Hear the strains of glorious anthems
  Coming from the Courts within;
Would you enter there, my brother,
  Then at once thyself prepare;
None but those who have the password
  Are allowed to enter There.
        Get the password, get the password,
          There is danger in delay;
        Hasten quickly, find the Master,
          He will tell thee what to say.

UNDER THE ROD.

I bow before Thee, O my God,
  In deep humility;
I ask Thee not to lift the rod
  That falls so hard on me;
Yet for this favor I would plead
  And fervently implore,
That Thou my wand'ring steps would lead
  To paths of peace once more.

That I have sinned I do confess;
  Thy laws have disobeyed,
And from the paths of righteousness
  I very far have strayed;
O turn my wand'ring steps about,
  My thoughts direct to Thee;
Dispel the clouds of sin and doubt,
  That hide Thee, Lord, from me.

Let not Thy hand more heavy fall
  Than I have strength to bear;
And give me grace to bear it all,
  Whatever be my share;
No mercy, Lord, can I demand
  Through merit of my own,
But yet I would Thy chast'ning hand
  Might fall on me alone.

Before Thy mercy seat I kneel,
  And on my bended knee,
Most earnestly do I appeal
  For loved ones dear to me;
That Thou wilt spare them, Lord, I trust,
  Whatever may befall;
That I should suffer is but just,
  Then let me suffer all.

I bow submissive to Thy will,
  Whate'er Thy will may be,
Believing that in mercy still
  Thou'lt lead me back to Thee;
But if Thy chast'ning I must bear
  Until my race is run,
O grant me faith in earnest prayer
  To say "Thy will be done."

COME AND FIND REST.

All ye by sin oppressed, weary and sore distressed,
  Why not in Jesus have faith and believe?
Be thy sins great or small, gladly He'll welcome all,
  None so unworthy He will not receive.

See how He stands and pleads, hear how He intercedes,
  Off'ring salvation abundant and free,
Come to the mercy seat, there kneel at Jesus' feet,
  Hear how He's calling, poor sinner, to thee.

Cast all thy doubts away, come without more delay,
    Come to the fountain that flows from His side,
Be thy sins what they may, all shall be washed away,
    Washed in the blood of the Savior who died.

Take all thy troubles there, fervently kneel in prayer,
    There all thy sorrows to Jesus make known,
Comfort he will impart, joy to the wounded heart,
    Jesus can save thee and Jesus alone.

Why will you longer stay?   Why will you still delay?
    Hasten, O, hasten to answer the call;   [are,
Though you have wandered far, come to Him as you
    Mercy and pardon He offers to all.

Come lay thy burdens down, come and accept a crown,
    Flee to the shelter that's found in His breast,
Cast all thy fears aside, come to the Crucified,
    Come and find comfort, salvation, and rest.

THE LOST SHEEP.

Far, far they have wandered away from the fold,
    Out on the bleak mountain so barren and cold,
Unsheltered from tempest, 'midst dangers unknown,
    Away from protection they wander alone.

They wander where pasture is not to be found,
    Where wolves in their hunger go prowling around,
The good shepherd calls them, but call as he may,
    The lost sheep, not hearing, go farther astray.

The rest of the flock are all safe in the fold,
    But woe to the lost ones exposed on the wold,
The good shepherd seeks them on mountain and plain,
    And constantly calls them, but calls them in vain.

Away from his care they have wandered afar,
    But dear to the shepherd the wanderers are;
He fain would have saved them, whatever the cost,
    But failing to find them he mourns for the lost.

'Tis thus with the sinner who wanders from God,
    He knows not the dangers that lie in his road;
Vain pleasures allure him, he revels in sin,
    And deeper and deeper he plunges therein.

Still onward, and downward, he follows the track,
    He hears not the voice that is calling him back;
He sees not the signal which to him that saith,
    "Before you lies danger, destruction and death."

No matter, O sinner, how lost you may feel,
    Thy wounds and thy bruises the Savior can heal,
Repentantly seek Him, rely on His love,
    And angels will greet thee with joy from above.

Though thy sins be as great as the mountains are high,
    He will make thee as pure as snow from the sky,
For none are so vile that he will not receive,
    If repentant they come, have faith, and believe.

TEACHINGS OF NATURE.

When morn proclaims by its approach
  That night has passed away,
The pow'r of God is then revealed
  In glorious light of day.

The sun in splendor we behold
  Ascending in the sky,
And in its brightness there we read
  Of Him who rules on high.

The little bird upon the bush
  That sits and sweetly sings,
Attunes its notes in praise of Him,
  The mighty King of Kings.

The flocks and herds that roam the plain,
  The insects in the sand,
And all the warbling feath'ry tribe,
  Bespeak the Maker's hand.

The gliding river, sparkling lake,
  The rippling little stream,
Show unto man the mighty work
  Of Him who reigns Supreme.

The forests, mountains, rocks and hills,
  All tell us at a glance,
That works of such magnificence
  Were never wrought by Chance.

The shady glens and flow'ry fields,
  The outstretched firmament;
All speak to us of One above,
  The great Omnipotent.

The raging storm, the tempest's howl,
  The sweet refreshing show'r,
Bear witness that there doth exist
  A great Controlling Power.

The lightning's red and lurid flash,
  The thunder's dreadful roll,
Are subject to the pow'r above,
  The God who rules the whole.

The radiant moon that shines at night,
  The sparkling stars on high,
Spring from the greater Source of Light
  That dwells above the sky.

The very air of which we breathe,
  Seas, oceans, lakes and land,
And all creations wondrous works,
  Show forth the Author's hand.

And man, with faculties so great
  And comprehensive mind,
Did he come forth a work of Chance,
  Or of the great Divine?

The sky above, the starry host,
  The earth by millions trod,
And all that are therein proclaim
  An everlasting God.

Go seek the depths of solitude,
  Where footsteps never trod,
And to thy heart a voice will speak,
  Declaring there's a God.

And thus we're taught from day to day,
  In all we see abroad,
That Nature's but the guiding post,
  That points us up to God.

A MEMORY.

It is only a cherished memory, but O, how sweet!
  And how often, in sad and lonely hours, it doth recall
The beautiful, angelic face I loved, and used to meet
  By the old ruined church, that stood with trembling,
        tott'ring wall.

That time of heavenly happiness, which was mine to
        share,
  Was too full of blissful joy to be of long duration;
And bright angels came, longing for her presence
        over There,   [lation.
  And called her home, leaving me in midst of deso-

'Tis only a memory! but to it I fondly cling,
  As closely as doth a loving wife to her nuptial ring;
And frequently I hear, as though 'twere wafted on
        the breeze,   [lost Therese.
  A sweet voice calling me, the voice of loved but

DEATHLESS LOVE.

O, how I loved her dear sweet face,
　　That ever brought such joy to me;
Her smile, her look, her angel voice,
　　Would fill my soul with ecstacy.

Perhaps to other eyes than mine,
　　She did not seem so fair to see;
But yet to me she always seemed
　　A reflex of divinity.

I loved her with as deep a love,
　　As earthly being could impart;
Nor time, nor space, nor circumstance,
　　Can ever take her from my heart.

That love to me she still returned,
　　Increased, at least, a thousand fold,
Nor change, nor place, nor act of mine,
　　Could ever make her love grow cold.

When act of folly I would do,
　　And others loudly would me blame,
She never lost her faith in me,
　　But loved me always just the same.

She would not wrongful act approve,
　　Or anything I did amiss;
But tempered judgment with her love,
　　And very often with a kiss.

I never wooed her for her hand,
　Although her heart was wholly mine;
But yet I loved and worshiped her,
　As one that might be deemed divine.

I loved her in my younger days,
　With all the ardor of my youth;
I loved her for herself alone—
　Embodiment of love and truth.

I loved her as the years rolled by,
　I love her still, though old and grey.
And nothing ever can arise
　To take my love from her away.

Although her brow is wrinkled now,
　And on her face no bloom I trace,
I love her just as tenderly
　As though bright youth adorned her face.

Each old grey hair upon her head,
　I hold more dear than costly gem;
And value more her silvered locks,
　Than coronet or diadem.

And yet the love I have for her,
　Campared with what she has for me,
Would bear no more comparison
　Than drop of water to the sea.

The lustre now has left her eyes,
　That once, like stars, shone bright and clear;
But Time nor Death, can ever end
　The deathless love of mother dear.

ALL MUST DIE.

All things that live must surely die,
  And some time pass away;
This is a law none can defy,
  But one all must obey.

The giant oak that rears its head,
  Above the rock bound shore;
The flow'rs that sweetest perfume shed.
  Must pass and be no more.

The little birds that sweetly sing;
  The flow'rs that bloom so gay;
And ev'ry living creeping thing,
  Must die and pass away.

The rose, however rich its bloom,
  Must wither and decay,
And man draws nearer to the tomb,
  On each succeeding day.

Yes, all must die, but how or when,
  We know not, can not say;
But ev'ry life must have an end,
  Come when, or how it may.

Death is the lot we all must share,
  And one by one we fall;
The old, the young, the brave, the fair,
  Must each obey the call.

Death severs ev'ry kindred tie,
　　None will the monster save;
As one by one the flowers die,
　　So men pass to the grave.

From loved ones we must separate,
　　To meet no more below;
And stricken hearts must mourn and wait,
　　'Till they are called to go.

'Tis hard when death's descending blow,
　　Falls on some darling's head,
And fills a mother's heart with woe,
　　And strikes some loved one dead.

And Oh! how hard to bear the stroke,
　　That sometimes on us fall,
To see the cords asunder broke,
　　That takes from us our all.

To rich and poor, to high and low,
　　Death's call is sure to come,
Then let us live, that when we go,
　　We'll find a better home.

VETERANS REUNION.

Brave vet'rans assembled, we meet once again,
　　Old scenes to review of the camp and the plain;
And incidents tell of that terrible strife,
　　When freedom was struggling and fighting for life.

This meeting for some may perhaps be the last,
　　And here as we talk and think over the past,
Emotions will rise which we cannot repel,
　　As comrades we think of who gallantly fell.

As here we're assembled our thoughts will revert,
　　To long dreary nights as we stood on alert;
To fields where we fought, as all freeman should do,
　　While fiercely contending the Gray with the Blue.

We'll hear the long roll, calling loudly—" To Arms,"
　　The bugle's shrill note, sending forth its alarms,
The booming of cannon, the rifles' report,
　　The loud ringing cheer as we charged on the fort.

And don't be surprised should we happen to hear,
　　The hiss of the bullet quite close to our ear;
Though rather unwelcome, it must be allowed,
　　When warned of its coming politely we bowed.

We'll think of the nights, midst the sleet and the snow,
　　As on picket we stood with face to the foe,
When the snap of a twig, bush moved by the air,
　　Caused trigger to say, " Come on, if you dare."

Varied scenes of the past, will rise up again,
  Some bringing us pleasure, some striking with pain,
But no scene half so sad, as when, side by side,
  We buried our comrades who gallantly died.

We laid them away without funeral rite,
  Coffinless, shroudless, as they fell in the fight,
Blood-stained and mangled, we buried them there,
  And gave them to earth without sermon or prayer.

No dear mother's kiss on the forehed was placed,
  No arms of a sweetheart the dying embraced,
No wife the fond husband to tenderly care,
  No sister to smooth out the blood-clotted hair.

As backward we look, saddended scenes will appear,
  And eyes will grow dim with the gathering tear,
Youthful forms we will see, in death sinking fast,
  And whisp'ring "Dear Mother," as breathing their
      last.

We well recollect how our hearts would rejoice,
  As "Mail" would be shouted in clear, ringing voice,
For nothing more welcome to soldier could come,
  Or bring him such joy as a letter from home.

The warrior's eye would betray his delight,
  At getting a letter some loved one did write;
Perhaps from dear mother, whose blessings it bore,
  Perhaps from a wife he would never see more.

While war had its hardships, its dangers and pain,
  Yet often both mirth and enjoyment would reign;
When heart moving song would be sung with a will,
  The sound coming back from the echoing hill.

Though hard was the struggle, as patriots we bore
  The hardships entailed, like our fathers of yore,
Who fought for their freedom on land and on sea,
  And proclaimed to the world: "Henceforth we are
    free."

When age dims our vision, and time frosts our hair,
  And we sit by the hearth in the old arm chair,
In sweet recollection, fond mem'ry shall dwell,
  On comrades who fought and heroically fell.

We see them to-day as they marched in the van,
  Courageous and fearless, and true to a man;
And which of us here but remembers with pride,
  How bravely they fought and courageously died.

For what did our comrades thus suffer and die,
  And lay down their lives without "wherefore" or
    "why"?
The answer is this: They gave all they could give,
  That Freedom, and Honor, and Country might live.

But where are the fruits of our victories now?
  The wreath has been torn from conqueror's brow,
And glorious achievements, unequaled before,
  Must now be forgotten and mentioned no more.

Blot out from the records the deeds of the past,
  Yet glory survives and shall live to the last;
And true we shall be till we muster Above,
  To the land we redeemed and flag that we love.

THE CONQUERED FLAG.

Now furl it, lay it in the dust,
Foul banner of a cause unjust,
For float again it never must,
    But ever buried be;
Banner beneath whose cursed waves,
Once lived a race of human slaves,
And sent to early, honored graves,
    Numberless of the free.

Flag of shame, forever fold it,
Never more let us behold it,
Cursed hands that e'er unrolled it,
    That we should ever see;
Unfurled from rampart's lofty height,
A banner black as shades of night,
Which traitors honored with delight,
    O'er that of liberty.

Now deeply let its grave be made,
In dark oblivion's darkest shade,
And there forever be it laid,
    To never rise again;
Down let it sink unknown to fame,
Wrapt up in infamy and shame,
Back to the regions whence it came,
    There ever to remain.

Supported by a dastard crew,
Traitors to flag and country too,
Who did their hands in blood imbue,
  And raised the rebel cry;
Banner beneath which traitors fought,
Foul banner stained with treason's spot,
Polluted banner, touch it not,
  Dishonored let it lie.

Broken is its staff and shattered,
Torn is now the flag and tattered,
Beaten too, and badly scattered,
  All its defenders are;
Not e'en a remnant let remain,
For traitor hands to raise again
Accursed banner raised in vain,
  In most unholy war.

Furl it now, unknown to glory,
Banner stigmatized in story,
Banner badly rent and gory,
  Deep sink it out of view;
Banner only scoffed and jeered at,
Once by traitors loudly cheered at,
Now by freemen only sneered at,
  We've seen the last of you.

Wave forth proud flag of liberty!
Float on, thou emblem of the free!
Wave o'er us still triumphantly,
  Though torn by many scars;
To nations far the tidings send,
Wherever freedom finds a friend,
That we will still our flag defend,
  The glorious Stripes and Stars.

OUR PATRIOT DEAD.

A DECORATION DAY POEM.

Thou Infinite Being, on whom we relied
    When proud hosts of treason against us were hurled,
Who conquered the haughty, and humbled their pride,
    And thus Freedom saved to enlighten the world.

For our Nation preserved, Thy name we adore,
    And ask that Thy blessing upon us be shed,
As here we're assembled, to render once more
    The tribute we owe to the heroic dead.

We bring to the place of their silent retreat,
    The sweetest of off'rings that can be bestowed,
Bright garlands to lay at their head and their feet,
    And flowers to cover their peaceful abode.

Step lightly and softly on this hallowed ground,
    Made sacred by those sleeping under its sod:
A patriot lies resting 'neath each little mound,
    A hero whose spirit now dwells with its God.

Though long since departed, their deeds we recall,
    As fighting for freedom we stood by their side,
While comrades around us, like leaves in the fall,
    Fell wounded and bleeding and gloriously died.

The soldier may fall in the midst of the fight,
    His proud, noble form to cold earth be consigned,
But they who fall fighting for Freedom and Right,
    In hearts of the brave shall be ever enshrined.

They are gone, aye, they're gone, we see them no more,
  In silence and sorrow we laid them away;
But back from the silent unmurmuring shore,
  Their voices are speaking to thousands to-day.

Though silent they sleep in their cold, narrow bed,
  They speak to us still from the regions above;
So tenderly soft is the voice of the dead,
  It comes like a zephyr, or whisper of love.

How calmly they sleep in their dwellings of rest,
  Who surrendered their lives that Freedom might
Still soft be the earth that lies over the breast. [live;
  Of those who for freedom gave all they could give.

The sun of their glory can never decline,
  While Time rolls along in its unceasing tide;
Resplendent in beauty forever shall shine,
  The bright star of those who for country have died.

When "grim visaged war" raised its threatening form,
  And great waves of treason dashed fiercely along,
As firm as a rock in the midst of the storm,
  They stood for the Right and resisted the Wrong.

Their love for the Union they sealed with their blood;
  To Freedom and Country were true to the end;
In forefront of battle they gallantly stood,
  The flag to protect and the nation defend.

Converse with the young on the battles they fought,
  And tell them the cause of the terrible strife;
Impress on their minds the grand lesson they taught,
  That Freedom and Honor are dearer than life.

Ah, well may we come with bright garlands to-day,
　To lay on the graves where the heroes now sleep;
We owe them a debt we can only repay,
　With love as profound as the ocean is deep.

Our vows of devotion here let us renew,
　As over their ashes sweet flowers we spread,
For naught more becomes a free people to do,
　Than garland the graves of the heroic dead.

By the land that they loved, redeemed at such cost;
　In mem'ry of those who so gallantly died;
Let enmities cease and war hatreds be lost
　In love for the flag that their blood purified.

We can, in true friendship, the right hand extend,
　And clasp that of him whom in combat we met;
Can hail him as "Brother," and greet him as "Friend,"
　But brave fallen comrades we cannot forget.

Sleep on, brave departed! in ages to come,
　The glory that crowns thee shall shine like a star;
Sleep on, undisturbed, neither trumpet nor drum,
　Shall wake thee again to the conflict of war.

Omnipotent power! whose name we adore,
　Increase our devotion to Country and Thee;
In sweet bonds of Union unite evermore,
　The North and the South 'neath the flag of the free.

FREEMEN, RISE

Rise, freemen, rise ! Be on your guard,
On Freedom's heights keep watch and ward,
Ominous sounds again are heard,
   Proclaiming danger near;
Canst thou not hear, as from afar,
The distant sounds of pending war,
And see above horizon's bar
   The gath'ring clouds appear?

Was it for naught ye fought and bled?
Was it for naught your comrades dead,
Breathed forth their last on gory bed
   That freedom might not die?
Is this the fruit ye thought to see
Reward your faith and loyalty,
That those ye conquered now should be
   Exalted up on high?

Who would have thought had it been told,
That we so shortly should behold,
Foul treason show a front so bold,
   Within the Congress halls;
Ye spirits of the patriots slain,
Must it be said ye died in vain,
That traitors now should rule again
   Within those honored walls.

Have ye forgot our patriot braves,
Whom traitors sent to early graves,
And shall we now submit as slaves,
  And of them pardon sue?
Were all our battles fought in vain?
For what were all our thousands slain?
That traitors now should us arraign,
  Because to country true.

O, woe the day, that we should see,
In this fair land of liberty,
Traitors rule triumphantly.
  Whom loyalty despise;
Was it for this so many died,
So many of their country's pride.
Whose bones are mould'ring side by side,
  Beneath the Southern skies!

Was it for this that heroes brave.
Whom mothers to their country gave.
And who, for freedom, found a grave,
  Or died in dismal pen?
Did Lincoln fall:—O stop and pause,
A martyr to the Union cause,
That traitors now should make the laws
  To govern loyal men?

Yet now they stalk, as once before.
In Congress halls, and on the floor
Declaim as in the days of yore,
  And boast with shouts of joy;
That records all expunged must be,
Which show their former infamy,
When fighting both on land and sea
  The Union to destroy.

FREEMEN, RISE!

And thus in their most bitter hate,
They undertake to dominate,
O'er those who conquered them of late,
  The gallant boys in Blue;
They think by other means to gain,
The cause for which they fought in vain,
And now upon another plan,
  The challenge they renew.

Shall we endure their scoffs and jeers,
Their boastful threats and taunting sneers,
We, who have saved by blood and tears,
  The flag we prize so high;
We feared them not when man for man,
We boldly met them hand to hand,
And still for our beloved land
  We conquer or we die.

If they the battle must renew,
A million freemen brave and true,
Once more will don the coat of Blue.
  Like gallant sons of Mars;
And with the banner of the free,
Proud emblem still of liberty.
Will march to glorious victory,
  Beneath the Stripes and Stars.

GENERAL W. T. SHERMAN.

IN MEMORIAM.

The chieftain now sleeps, and the sound of the drum
 Will wake him no more by its sudden alarms;
The gallant commander no longer will come,
 When heroes are summoned to gird on their arms;
His sword, so triumphant, no more will be drawn,
 Returned to its scabbard, it hangs on the wall;
The soldier, the hero, the patriot is gone,
 And sadly the nation mourns over his fall.

No more will his figure appear on parade,
 Or smile on the troops as they pass in review;
" Break ranks " was the order, he heard and obeyed,
 And stepped out of line as a soldier should do;
No more will his form, so majestic and grand,
 At head of the column march proudly to war;
No more in the midst of the battle he'll stand,
 Inspiring his soldiers, like Prince of Navarre.

Brave comrades who often have fought by his side,
 Will grieve that their gallant commander's no more;
He whom they had followed with courage and pride,
 To glorious achievements, unequaled before;
They'll think of the time, in the years that are gone,
 When in battle they stood, with him at their head;
They will see him again dash fearlessly on,
 'Midst volleys of shrapnel and showers of lead.

Scenes almost forgotten will rise up again,
  Recalling the brave, who heroically died;
Dead, dying, and wounded, they'll see on the plain,
  The forms of dear comrades who fell by their side;
As war's panorama unfolds to their gaze,
  Scenes brighter and grander will often appear;
Again freedom's standard, in triumph they'll raise,
  'Mid salvos of cannon, and loud ringing cheer.

Again "Chattanooga" will pass in review,   [Ridge;"
  And "Shiloh," and "Corinth," and "Rocky Face
And "Memphis," and "Hindman," and "Grenada" too,
  And "Dallas," and "Ringgold," and "Black River
"Resaca," and "Kenesaw Mount" will appear, [Bridge;"
  And close to "Atlanta," "Savannah" will be;
And then will be heard the victorious cheer,
  That greeted the world famous "March to the Sea."

No wonder that veterans' eyes should grow dim;
  No wonder in sorrow their heads they should bend;
Brave comrades in arms, ever faithful to him,
  And true to the cause he did nobly defend;
To each and to all he was ever endeared,
  No Chieftain so honored and loved as was he;
And ever by them will his name be revered,
  While river continues to flow to the sea.

Though valiant in battle, and fearless in fight,
  Yet still from his heart would sweet tenderness flow;
Though firm and unyielding while standing for right,
  His hand would in friendship clasp that of a foe;
Though brave as a lion when danger was near
  And death dealing bullets went flying through space,
The battle once ended, again would appear
  The goodness and kindness that beamed in his face.

Though soldier so great, never harsh or unkind;
  In speech ever gentle, respectful, and frank;
His high soul of honor, and pureness of mind,
  Endeared him to those of inferior rank;
No blemish or spot ever tarnished his name,
  And pure was his life from beginning to end;
Though highly exalted in honor and fame,
  He ever stood ready the poor to befriend.

Unbending he stood in defense of the right,
  And firm as a rock in opposing the wrong;
Though lover of peace, ever ready to fight
  The weak to defend when assailed by the strong;
No airs of the haughty he ever put on;
  In ranks of true manhood he stood in the van;
Though covered with honors heroically won,
  His greatness consisted in being a Man.

As soldier, proud Cæsar was famous in war;
  Like bright flashing meteor, Napoleon sprang forth;
The world was illumined by Wellington's star,
  But equally great was the son of the North;
If heroes are measured by what they have done,
  Then Sherman should high on the list be enrolled;
The battles he fought, and the vict'ries he won,
  Entitle his name to be written in gold.

But now he has answered his final tattoo;
  He's gone to be mustered with heroes above,
Where thousands of comrades, brave, noble and true,
  Will meet him and hail him with greetings of love.
Though 'Lights Out' have sounded, and all through the
  The order has passed to extinguish the 'glim,' [camp,
The bright star of Sherman, like heavenly lamp,
  Will shine on for ever, it cannot grow dim.

Though comrades will miss him when mustering here.
　　Yet still on the roll will his name be displayed;
In bright golden letters 'twill always appear,
　　And he'll be "accounted for" still at parade;
Though ages in rapid succession may fly,
　　Till systems all verge on eternity's shore;
The glory that crowned him will fade not or die,
　　Till sounds the last trumpet and Time is no more.

Though beautiful flowers may garland his grave,
　　And over his ashes shed sweetest perfume;
In hearts of the loyal, the true, and the brave,
　　His name will be kept in perpetual bloom;
Cold marble may crumble and moulder to dust,
　　And high polished granite may tumble to waste;
And bronze may decay from exposure and rust,
　　But not from the heart can his name be erased.

Departed Commander! now camped on the shore,
　　Where Prince of all Peace is supreme in command;
How soon thy brave comrades will follow thee o'er,
　　And join thee again in that beautiful land;
They're rapidly nearing the end of the march,
　　And all the old vet'rans will shortly be gone;
A few years at farthest, and under the arch,
　　The last one will pass to the muster Beyond.

YOU TELL.

They left their homes and firesides,
 And dear ones loved so well,
And went as gallant volunteers
 To fight for what?   You tell.

They kissed the loved ones all good-by;
 Then spoke the sad farewell;
And marched like heroes to the war,
 To fight 'gainst whom?   You tell.

Through summer heat and winter cold,
 They marched o'er hill and dell;
And often slept upon the snow,
 In cause of what?   You tell.

Though hunger's pangs they often felt,
 No murmurs from them fell;
And sufferings untold they bore,
 And all for what?   You tell.

They felt the agonies of thirst;
 They faced both shot and shell;
Above the clouds they bravely fought,
 To conquer what?   You tell.

They stormed the ramparts threat'ning hights
 With loud victorious yell;
And braved the cannon's flaming mouth,
 Defending what?   You tell.

They suffered cruelties untold,
  In dungeon and in cell;
And vermin fattened on their flesh,
  Because they what?   You tell.

In prison they have undergone
  Worse tortures than in hell;
Maltreated, starved, shot down like dogs,
  For doing what?   You tell.

Bloodhounds pursued them thro' the woods,
  And chased them o'er the fell;
All tortures demons could devise
  They suffered.   Why?   You tell.

They fought as only heroes fight,
  And thousands of them fell;
And for the blood so freely shed,
  What have they now?   You tell.

All these they bravely underwent,
  Foul treason to repel;
But has the flag been saved or not?
  Perhaps it has.   You tell.

For battles fought and vict'ries won,
  What have the victors now?
For country saved and flag redeemed,
  What laurels crown their brow?
               You tell.

HE'LL NOT BE ON THE TRAIN TO-DAY.

When treason sought by act of war
  The Union to disintegrate,
A German, named Von Isenberg,
  Resided in the Keystone state.
Peace dwelt within his humble home,
  And there with true, devoted wife,
And loving children round his hearth,
  He lived a peaceful, happy life.

Up from the South in might and pow'r,
  Disloyal legions sallied forth,
Led by the sons of chivalry,
  To fight against the loyal North.
The country's flag they tore in shreds,
  And trampled it beneath their feet;
And more to emphasize their hate,
  They dragged it through the filthy street.

But when the flag of liberty,
  They undertook to desecrate,
Von Isenberg resolved to go,
  And fight for freedom, flag and State.
Dark om'nous clouds were gath'ring fast,
  And people viewed them from afar;
And thought in them they saw a sign,
  That told of fearful civil war.

What sound was that, but faintly heard,
  Like rumbling thunder passing by?
What meant that meteoric flash
  That, swift as lightning, swept the sky?
Too soon their dread portent was known;
  They presaged scenes of fearful strife;
They told the dreadful die was cast,
  On which would hang the nation's life.

When to his wife the German told,
  ·That for the war he meant to start;
She felt a pain shoot through her breast,
  As though an arrow pierced her heart.
But like true heroine she bore
  The fearful stroke that had been dealt;
She did not seek to ward it off,
  Nor did she show the pain she felt.

But when the time to part arrived,
  She could not well suppress her fears;
Nor could see, by her force of will,
  Keep down her sighs and rising tears.
She only said:—"I nevermore
  Shall see your face this side the grave;"
But he responded with a kiss,
  And told her that she must be brave.

No braver man e'r drew a sword,
  Or took a rifle in his hand;
And soon, by merit of his worth,
  He had a comp'ny to command.
But time sped onward in its flight,
  And two long years had passed, and more,
Since he had parted with his wife,
  And left her weeping at the door.

"As pants the heart for water brooks,"
  So yearned his soul once more to see,
The loving wife and little ones,
  Of whom he thought so tenderly.
How many comrades he recalled,
  Who fell while fighting by his side,
Whose loved ones now were left to mourn,
  The loss of those who nobly died.

The leave for which he had applied,
  No sooner did he it obtain,
Than to his wife he wrote and said
  That she might meet him at the train.
But when the joyful news was sent,
  How little thought the soldier then,
That she to whom the tidings went,
  Would never see his face again.

Next day the rebels stormed the works,
  Where he was stationed with his men,
And having entered in the fight,
  All thought of home was banished then.
His place was in the foremost rank,
  Resisting charges made in vain,
Until a bullet pierced his heart,
  And stretched him lifeless on the plain.

In freedom's cause he nobly fell,
  While fighting like a hero brave,
And now the flag he loved so well,
  Floats proudly o'er his honored grave.
And thus for his adopted land,
  To prove how great the love he bore,
He gave his life a sacrifice,
  What noble patriot could do more?

The train arrived, the wife was there,
　But him she looked for, where was he?
She saw the thronging crowds desperse,
　But him she sought she did not see.
Awhile she stood when all had gone,
　Then turning, sadly moved away,
Repeating in a saddened voice,
　"He'll not be on the train to day."

Day after day she still would go,
　To meet his coming on the train;
Alas, poor soul she did not know
　He ne'er would smile on her again.
Hope from her heart began to flee,
　And then, despairing, she would say,
"He never, never will return,
　He'll not be on the train to-day."

At length she heard the painful news,
　Of how her husband had been slain,
And arrow piercing through her heart,
　Could not have caused her greater pain.
Her grief no language can express;
　Her mind became a total wreck,
And ever since that mournful day,
　She roams about a maniac.

By night and day she still is seen,
　In storm and sunshine, snow and rain,
Most sadly pacing to and fro,
　While waiting for the looked for train.
And still the mournful wail is heard,
　As she in sorrow moves away;
"I wonder why he does not come,
　He'll not be on the train to-day."

Though many years have come and gone,
　She ceases not her watch to keep;
But while she waits and watches there,
　The one she seeks is sound asleep.
Her hair, once black as raven's wing,
　Its color shortly changed to grey,
But still she waits, and still she sighs,
　"He'll not be on the train to-day."

WHAT'S THE MATTER, MAUD?

Pray tell me where the matter lies,
　That you'll not send a line;
Am I turned hateful to your eyes,
　Or banished from your mind?

If any cause to thee I gave,
　Whereat you took offense,
A thousand pardons here I crave,
　And plead my ignorance.

Perhaps some villain's poisoned thee
　With stories false and base;
I dare the wretch, whoe'er he be,
　To meet me face to face.

A truer lover never wooed
  Than I have been to thee;
And hence your silent attitude
  Is great surprise to me.

Could I but know, e'en for thy sake,
  Why thus you are inclined,
I then perhaps might undertake
  To disabuse your mind.

But why you should me thus afflict,
  Is all unknown to me;
Have I been false or derilect,
  Or faithless unto thee?

The cause of this strange, sudden turn,
  I really can't surmise,
But that by you I should be spurned,
  Has caused me some surprise.

It may be that you now regret
  The vows to me conveyed;
And that you're striving to forget,
  The promises you made.

Why, bless your heart, if that is so,
  You need not troubled be;
For I will only be too glad
  To thus get rid of thee.

I sometimes think you only sought
  To use me as a "tool,"
And that you entertain the thought
  That I am but a fool.

Against what you may think or do,
 I set up no defense;
But when I loved a *thing* like you,
 I showed my want of sense.

Don't think I'll weep and mourn for thee,
 Like love-sick, simple swain;
I'll cast my net into the sea
 And try my luck again.

TO ANGELINE.

Since first my eyes did rest on thee,
 My heart was altogether thine;
No other e'er so dear to me
 As thou, my once loved Angeline.

My ev'ry thought thou wert by day,
 Thy image ever on my mind;
Be where I might, my thoughts would stray
 Forever back to Angeline.

Thy charming face so fair to see,
 And eyes that, diamond like, didst shine,
Didst fill my heart with love for thee,
 A love cast off by Angeline.

And yet you led me to believe
　　Thy love you gave for that of mine;
But basely thou didst me deceive,
　　O fair but fickle Angeline.

The love I bore thee none can tell;
　　My ev'ry tender thought was thine;
Too late I see I loved too well
　　The faithless, heartless Angeline.

O woe the day when thee I met,
　　That now all hope I must resign;
Henceforth I'll struggle to forget
　　The false, deceitful Angeline.

FORSAKEN.

He told me that his love was mine,
　　And said that I should be his bride,
And I, believing, trusted him,
　　And in his honor did confide.
The love I bore him none can tell,
　　And dear to me he soon became;
Eternal love he vowed to me
　　By ev'ry fond endearing name.

He spoke to me so lovingly,
   And said that nothing should us part;
And ev'ry loving word he spoke
   Found resting place within my heart.
So tenderly he told his love,
   While I, enraptured, sat and heard,
And listened with such fond delight,
   Believing then his ev'ry word.

He loved but me and me alone,
   None else his love should ever share;
And like an unsuspecting bird
   I fell into the tempter's snare.
But I discovered, all too late,
   That he was false to ev'ry vow,
And for the love I gave to him,
   I'm outcast and forsaken now.

FAREWELL TO JENNIE.

The time has come when I must say
   The parting word 'tween you and me,
But wander where my footsteps may,
   I still shall fondly think of thee.

Since cruel fate decrees it so,
   That now forever we must part,
I leave with thee before I go
   The fondest wish of loving heart.

My fate seems hard, but I shall strive
    To bear whatever may befall;
"For better 'tis to love and lose,
    Than know I had not loved at all."

When Death approached with silent tread,
    And took from me my Adelaine,
I thought love's passion then was dead,
    And never hoped to love again.

But thou the embers didst revive,
    And in my heart I felt the glow
Of love rekindled and alive
    With all the warmth of years ago.

Once more it's dying, dying fast,
    The flame you lit is sinking low;
My fate is sealed, the die is cast,
    And sadly now from thee I go.

When I am gone, my earnest prayer
    Shall ever to the Throne ascend,
That He who reigns in mercy there,
    May thee protect and still defend.

No envious thought invades my mind,
    Because thy love I cannot share;
And since all hope I must resign,
    That God may bless thee is my prayer.

May all that tends to comfort thee,
    Forever, Jennie, with thee dwell;
And ever thou'lt remembered be
    By him who bids thee now farewell.

THE NEGLECTED WIFE.

Is this the joy I was to share,
  The bliss of wedded life?
Is this the faith he vowed to me
  When I should be his wife?
O fatal love ! O trusting heart !
  How soon to sorrow known,
That here in solitude I weep
  Neglected and alone.

I little thought when I with him
  Before the altar stood,
That he would leave me here alone
  To weep in solitude;
Have all the charms he once extolled
  From me so quickly fled?
Or must I think—O God forbid—
  His love for me is dead?

How he was wont to sit by me,
  And think it bliss supreme;
But now that time to me appears
  Like some delightful dream;
Or like a snowflake on the lake,
  Or dew-drop 'neath the sun,
Or like the last expiring breath
  Of one whose race is run.

Is this to be my hopeless fate
　　Through all the coming years,
That I'm to sit alone and hold
　　Companionship with tears?
He goes from me I know not where,
　　I do not ask him why;
Nor does he ever seem to see
　　The tear-drop in my eye.

He does not seem to realize
　　The bitter cup I drink;
And for the heart that loves him still
　　He does not seem to think;
O cruel, cruel, cruel fate,
　　How wretched is the life
Of her who sits and weeps alone,
　　The true, neglected wife.

"It is not all of life to live,
　　Nor all of death to die;"
Nor is it all of wedded life
　　The household to supply;
A loving kiss, a tender word,
　　A fond and dear caress,
Will make the peasant's humble cot
　　A home of pleasantness.

He thinks that I should be content,
　　As I am well supplied;
And that because he pays the bills
　　I should be satisfied;
But there is one thing he forgets,
　　That stands all else above,
That nothing in the world beside
　　Can take the place of love.

Night after night alone I sit
  And count the striking bell;
And hear the watchman on his rounds
  Proclaim that "All is well;"
And as the midnight hour I hear,
  I answer with a moan,
To think that I am left to sit
  Neglected and alone.

With painful heart I seek my couch,
  But not to go to sleep,
For there, in utter loneliness,
  I only sob and weep;
And there, from my disordered brain,
  Strange fantasies will rise;
And horrid spectres will appear
  And stand before my eyes.

I hear a footstep on the walk
  And wonder if 'tis he;
It does not stop, but passes on,
  And then the clock strikes Three.
O joyless life! O wretched wife!
  Had I but only known,
That I so soon should sit and weep
  Neglected and alone.

KISSING IN THE DARK.

One ev'ning strolling carelessly
   Along the darkened street,
By some mistake, as I supposed,
   A female did me greet.

"Good ev'ning, sir," to me she said,
   And such was my reply,
And then she made a sudden stop,
   And likewise so did I.

Her countenance I tried to see,
   But all my efforts failed,
And, as to hide it still the more,
   She had it closely veiled.

"Perhaps you'll think it rude of me
   That I should you accost,
But, really sir, I must confess
   I rather fear I'm lost."

"Indeed," said I, "that is too bad,
   Pray, where do you reside?"
"I'm stopping out on Waltham Road,"
   She modestly replied.

"The Waltham Road?   Then true it is
   That you have gone astray;
Your footsteps you must turn about
   And go the other way.

"O, dear," she rather sighed than said,
  And then she did remark,
"I really am afraid to go
  The night's so very dark."

Just what to do in such a case,
  To me was not quite clear;
Should I, as act of gallantry,
  My service volunteer.

Then came the thought, "is this a trap,
  Or is it as she said?"
"Whichever way it is," thought I,
  "I'll offer her my aid."

"Madam," I said, "if you desire,
  Your escort I will be;"
"O, sir," said she, "you do not know
  The joy you give to me."

Her tongue was smooth, her voice was sweet,
  Her speech extremely bland;
Nor did I think it out of place
  To take her by the hand.

It seemed as though she'd never cease
  To thank me on the way,
And said to me, "your kindness, sir,
  I never can repay."

"You overrate the courtesy
  Too much, I am afraid,
But let me only press thy lips
  And I shall be repaid."

"If that is all you ask," said she,
  "For service such as this,
I cannot well refuse to grant
  The pleasure of a kiss."

Her home was reached, and at the gate
  Her hand I did resign;
"Won't you step in?" she said to me,
  "You've been so very kind."

With kiss yet burning on my lips,
  And heart set all aglow,
When she the invitation gave
  I could not answer No.

No sooner was the veil removed
  Than I made for the door,
For there I saw a colored wench
  Stand smiling on the floor.

Now that you know how I was fooled, .
  Just let me here remark,
Be sure you know whose lips you press
  When kissing in the dark.

WHAT IS IT TO YOU?

If I go out to take a ride
  In buggy or in chaise,
And I have sitting by my side
  A girl with handsome face;
And if, as on we gaily go,
  I steal a kiss or two,
And should my arm around her throw,
  Pray, what is it to you?

If I meet lady young and fair,
  And offer her my arm,
And she accepts it then and there,
  It surely is no harm;
Should I invite her to the park,
  The sights and scenes to view,
And there we enter on a lark,
  Pray, what is it to you ?

If at a ball by chance I see
  A girl inclined to chat,
And she should dance or waltz with me,
  There's nothing wrong in that;
Should I with her perambulate,
  As lads and lasses do,
And leave her smiling at the gate,
  Pray, what is it to you?

Should I go sleighing with a lass,
   And she should not decline
To let my arm around her pass,
   What bus'ness is't of thine?
Or if, while on the rink we be,
   I stoop to tie her shoe,
And should her pretty ankle see,
   Pray, what is it to you?

If in the woods I chance to stray
   With handsome, merry lass,
And we, to while the time away,
   Should sit upon the grass;
And I should take her to my arms,
   As lovers often do,
And yield to her bewitching charms,
   Pray, what is it to you?

What right have you to stick your nose,
   And sneak 'round on the sly,
To pry out what your neighbor does,
   And act the part of spy?
What right have you to interfere,
   With what your neighbors do?
Should they drink water, wine or beer,
   Pray, what is it to you?

I think the better plan would be,
   Were it but practiced more,
If busy-folks would try to see
   The dirt behind *their* door.
If you but mind your own affairs,
   You'll find enough to do,
And though I should neglect my prayers,
   Pray, what is it to you?

CHICAGO DAY AT WORLD'S FAIR.

WORLD'S FAIR, 1893.

O the hustling and the bustling,
  And swaying to and fro;
And the hurry and the flurry
  As crowds would come and go;
And the ramming and the cramming,
  And jostling ev'rywhere;
And the flutt'ring and the sputt'ring,
  In getting to the Fair.

O the rushing and the crushing,
  And squeezing to get through;
And the aching and the quaking
  As pressure stronger grew;
How they weltered and they sweltered
  And struggled to get there,
For all were bent with strong intent
  That they would reach the Fair.

O the howling and the growling
  As crowds would closer pack;
And the screaming and blaspheming
  As they were driven back;
For broken shin or rib caved in
  They did not seem to care;
They'd stand the thumps and bear the bumps
  But could not miss the Fair.

O the snatching and the scratching
   And sudden shrieks of pain;
And the stumbling and the tumbling
   In getting to the train;
Good Deacons swore who ne'er before
   Were ever known to swear;
And words would slip from Sister's lip
   She would not use in prayer.

The women scowled and fiercely growled
   As "rip" their dress would go;
And men enraged became engaged
   In giving blow for blow;
Lunch boxes all were pulverized,
   The pastry all was smashed,
And pie and cake and sandwiches
   Were all together mashed.

They scrambled over balustrades,
   They climbed up over sheds,
And some would undertake to walk
   On top of people's heads;
They crowded all the tramway cars,
   And still they came in flocks,
And on the steamboats they were packed
   Like herring in a box.

The railway trains were crammed so full
   Men could not turn around;
They stood as thick on cable cars
   As leaves lie on the ground;
To reach the "L" one might as well
   Attempt to stem the tide;
Stop the motion of the ocean
   Or mountains cast aside.

Conveyances of ev'ry kind,
　　Of ev'ry make and hue,
In taking people to the Fair
　　Had more than they could do;
They went in Omnibus and Hack,
　　The Tally-Hoes were jammed,
In lumber wagons they were packed,
　　And Herdics all were crammed.

Like huge billows of the ocean
　　That in succession roll,
So onward moved the human tide
　　Still surging tow'rd the goal;
Beholders stood with bated breath
　　And looked on with dismay,
As people crowded to the Fair
　　Upon Chicago Day.

MY THREE-YEAR-OLD.

She is a cherub bright and fair,
　　With eyes as blue as blue can be;
And how the little elf can climb,
　　Is really wonderful to see.
Sometimes on table-top she'll perch,
　　And next I'll see her on the shelf;
I'm kept on nettles all the time,
　　Lest she should fall and kill herself.

But then she is so sweet and "cute,"
　With pretty yellow, golden curls,
And then her white and shiny teeth,
　Are like so many little pearls.
But full of mischief too is she,
　And things will do which I forbid,
But yet I would not hurt the "tot,"
　No matter what the darling did.

When dish she breaks, or milk upsets,
　Or on the carpet spills her food,
She looks so innocent and sweet,
　I cannot scold her if I would.
And oft a saint it would provoke,
　To see the tricks she will perform,
But one look from her little eyes,
　Will drive away the rising storm.

Sometimes from home she runs away,
　And wanders from the neighborhood,
And then her father almost swears,
　And says, "I'll spank the mischief good."
But when at length she toddling comes,
　The spanking threats have left his head,
And then he runs and picks her up,
　And gives her kisses in their stead.

Sometimes my temper's sorely tried,
　To see her coming from the street,
With face and hands bedaubed with mud,
　And mud all o'er from head to feet.
I feel that I could shake her "good,"
　If the mischief only knew it,
But when I see her little tears,
　I have not the heart to do it.

No matter what the toy she has,
 She never will be satisfied,
Until she picks it all apart,
 To see what it has got inside.
The tricks of mischief she will play,
 A very saint would aggravate,
Now striking matches on the wall,
 Next lighting paper at the grate.

Her Pa's revolver once she found,
 Where it lay loaded on the stand,
And out she came into room,
 Displaying it as something grand.
"Bang, bang," she cried, as playing "shoot,"
 While I sat breathless at the sight,
And for a time I could not move,
 So paralyzed was I with fright.

Up to the bureau once she climbed,
 And ere the mischief I could stop,
She had her father's razor out,
 Hammering on the marble-top.
If child was e'er to mischief born,
 And such would seem to be the case,
That child must surely then be mine,
 Although it shows not in her face.

But who can blame the little things?
 They mean no harm, do what they may;
Just think how cheerless home would be.
 Without some darling there to play.
For all the mischief that she makes,
 I would not for a world of gold,
Exchange my aggravating elf,
 My darling little three-year-old.

MY BRIAR ROOT.

It consoles me in my sadness,
　　It soothes me in my pain;
It is my greatest comforter
　　When trouble's on the brain;
When I brood in melancholy,
　　And burdened am with grief,
'Tis then my dear old briar root
　　Affords me great relief.

When my mind is in a muddle,
　　And my thoughts are all astray
My boon companion I take up,
　　And puff dull care away;
When troubles great do me oppress,
　　And sorrow is my share,
My briar root comes to my aid,
　　And lifts me from despair.

When my wife commences scolding,
　　And gives her tongue its play;
I take my dear old briar root
　　And let her scold away;
And while she raves about the house,
　　And calls me for a brute;
I always keep my temper down,
　　With dear old briar root.

When bored to death with this and that,
　And feel like raising Cain;
There's nothing calms like briar root
　My half demented brain;
When disappointed creditors,
　Stand cursing on the stair,
I keep quite cool with briar root,
　And let them rant and swear.

When my best laid plans miscarry,
　As oft they do, of course,
I consult my old companion,
　And say it might be worse;
And here, with bumper to the brim,
　My friend I now salute,
And pledge myself to never part
　With dear old briar root.

JOHN AND SALLY'S COURTSHIP.

John courted Sally three long years,
　And loved her as his life;
A single thought he never had
　But that she'd be his wife;
To him had Sally often vowed,
　She surely would him wed,
And he, in his simplicity,
　Believed what Sally said.

As token of their plighted troth,
　Like lover true and brave,
He bought a very handsome ring
　Which he to Sally gave;
They calmly sailed the stream of love,
　And John felt satisfied
That willing answer she would give,
　When asked to be his bride.

But when three years had passed away,
　And John did not propose,
She wondered if he ever meant
　The courting term to close;
She tried in many little ways
　To lead him to the point,
But by the time she got him there,
　His tongue was out of joint.

She ventured once to go so far,
　While standing at the gate,
To call to mind, that soon the birds
　Would all begin to mate;
But still he paused, nor did he see
　How scornful was her glance,
Because he did not take the hint,
　To make the least advance.

Then Sally's love began to wane,
　She could not see the use
Of wasting all her time and love
　On such a stupid goose;
"I wonder what the gawky means?
　His conduct is so queer;
Does he suppose I'll wait, and wait,
　On him year after year?"

While in this troubled state of mind,
   A stranger came along;
A dashing fel ow, too, was he,
   Whose name was Mr. Strong.
To Sally he was introduced,
   And soon she came to know,
That fault with him she could not find,
   About his being slow.

The new acquaintance thus sprung up
   Advanced at rapid pace,
And while she sometimes thought of John,
   He fast was losing place;
But still in his peculiar way,
   He played the lover's part,
But Strong was fast supplanting him
   In Sally's love and heart.

That Sally would not marry him,
   John never once supposed,
But courage he could never find,
   To have the bargain closed,
If he had only had the nerve,
   His suit he might have won;
But three years courtship, Sally thought,
   Was long enough for fun.

At length one day he did resolve,
   To cast all fears aside,
And boldly started off to ask
   If she would be his bride;
Dressed in his best he took the road,
   Nor did he once suspect,
When he the question would propound,
   That she would him reject.

With joyful heart he lightly walked,
    Repeating as he went
The speech that he would make to her,
    When asking her consent.
But now his heart begins to beat,
    Much faster than before;
And strange sensations o'er him steal
    As nearing Sally's door.

He wiped his face, smoothed down his hair,
    His vest he did adjust;
Then from his boots, with handkerchief
    He brushed away the dust.
Advancing then, he gave a knock;
    No answer came thereto,
Behind the curtain Sally stood,
    The window peeping through.

Short space he stood, then knocked again,
    Much louder than before;
When Sally, beaming o'er with smiles,
    Went skipping to the door.
"Why, John!" and then she dropped her voice,
    "Where have you been so long?
Come in, and you'll be pleased I know,
    To meet with Mr. Strong."

But ling'ring there he mutely stood,
    Like one that's lost in doubt;
At length with falt'ring voice he asked
    If Sally would come out.
"Sally," he said, then dumb was he,
    His further speech was gone;
But she, in sympathetic tone,
    Said, "What's the matter, John?"

Right in his throat a lump arose,
  The sweat ran down his cheek;
He wiped his forehead, gave a cough,
  And then he tried to speak.
"Sally, you know," and then he stopped;
  "Know what?" said she, "go on;"
"You know that I"—a pause, she smiled,
  "I what?" she asked of John.

"For three long years have courted you
  And loved you as my life,
And now, my darling, I have come,
  To ask you for my wife."
"Your wife, why John, do you not know
  That I am Mrs. Strong?
Hereafter, when you want to wed,
  You must not court so long."

PULL THE CURTAINS DOWN.

How many are the saddened hearts
  That grief and sorrow share;
How many are the ruined lives
  A prey to dark despair;
How many are the homes destroyed
  Where peace and joy were found,
And all because they did not think
  To pull the curtains down.

How many things in secret done
   Might never come to light,
If those by whom they are enjoyed
   Would only use their sight,
And see the curtains were pulled down
   To shut them in from view,
And thus prevent some other eyes
   From seeing what they do.

How many budding charms of maid
   Might never be exposed,
If they would only take the thought
   To have the shutters closed;
If they but knew while posturing,
   And pirouetting round,
That other eyes were watching them,
   They'd pull the curtains down.

Young ladies oft before the glass
   Stand looking at their charms,
And practice many attitudes
   Displaying legs and arms,
They little think that other eyes
   Look on with great delight,
And 'cause the curtains are not down
   Are feasting on the sight.

They ought to read their Bible more,
   And always bear in mind
What happened to Uriah's wife
   In good old Palestine;
But had she, when she went to bathe,
   But pulled the curtains down,
She never would have borne a son
   To wear King David's crown.

And older ladies oft neglect
  To act with prudent care,
And show themselves in attitudes
  Not oft assumed in prayer;
And often they denude themselves
  From chemisette to gown,
Unmindful that they had forgot
  To pull the curtains down.

And preachers, too, are sometimes caught
  Engaged in the pursuit
Of prowling 'round the orchard wall
  To steal forbidden fruit;
They do not seem to have a thought
  For either cross or crown;
And venture to approach the tree
  With curtains not pulled down.

A modest man would turn aside,
  Nor stop to feast his eyes
On charms not meant for him to see,
  Which women dearly prize;
But men are human after all,
  And women are the same;
And if the curtains are not down
  Perhaps they're not to blame.

What scandal might be overcome
  And never brought to light,
If people only would but think
  To close the shutters tight,
If they must kiss, why, let them kiss,
  And clasp each other round,
But then it might be just as well
  To pull the curtains down.

Oft people learn to their surprise,
　　That things they did alone,
In secret, too, as they supposed,
　　Are pretty widely known;
But in their own forgetfulness
　　The explanation's found;
They did not think, when in their room,
　　To pull the curtains down.

God gave us ears that we might hear,
　　And eyes that we might see,
And women He endowed with charms
　　Angelic in degree;
And he who views them unconcerned
　　Is either fool or clown,
And hasn't sense enough himself
　　To pull the curtains down.

TOILERS OF AMERICA.

O ye who well might once proclaim
　　To all the world that ye were free,
To whom through patriot blood there came
　　The priceless gem of liberty;
Ye whose fathers still defended
　　Fair freedom's cause on land and sea;
Ye from heroes loins descended,
　　What freedom now is left to thee?

Freedom from you hath departed,
  Her throbbing pulse no more you feel,
Prone she lies and broken hearted,
  Her neck beneath the tyrant's heel.
Not one single arm defends her,
  As wounded, bleeding there she lies;
Not one helping hand befriends her,
  While cowards watch her as she dies.

O ye base, degenerate race,
  Must Freedom prostrate, helpless lie,
While ye look on with sullen face,
  And see her suffer, bleed, and die?
Shall Freedom call to you in vain,
  As she with dying voice departs?
Does not one patriot spark remain,
  To kindle up your coward hearts?

Unworthy sons of noble sires,
  To see fair Freedom stricken low,
While ye stand by as she expires,
  And dare not strike one single blow.
O what utter, vile subjection
  Has come upon this noble race,
Freedom dies without protection,
  And tyranny usurps her place.

In this her hour of sorest need,
  Do thou O God, that rules on high,
Extend thine arm and intercede,
  And do not let fair Freedom die.
Protect her with thy mighty hand,
  And raise her bleeding form again,
And make these cravens understand,
  That to be free they must be men.

A noble people once were ye,
   Whose valor made you world renowned,
But former glory's passed from thee,
   And now in fetters ye are bound.
Your old-time martial spirit's dead,
   And ye submit to sordid knaves;
Valor, pride, and manhood's fled,
   And ye no better are than slaves.

Ye bend the neck to bear the yoke,
   And groan beneath the heavy load;
Submissively ye take the stroke
   Of tyrant's lash, or pointed goad.
Indignities you undergo,
   However much to your dislike,
Ye take the vile, insulting blow,
   But, coward like, ye dare not strike.

Yet still ye boast of being free,
   And freedom's banner o'er ye waves,
Yet not a land across the sea,
   Contains a baser race of slaves.
Does this your freedom constitute,
   Your manly independence show,
That ye, like more courageous brute,
   Would kiss the hand that strikes the **blow?**

The circuit of the earth go round,
   From frigid zone to dark Soudan,
And viler slaves will not be found,
   Than in this christian governed land.
Mean slaves to tyrants harsh control;
   Slaves enlinked to want and woe;
Slaves enfettered hand and soul;
   Slaves in degradation low;

Slaves to wealth and corporations,
   Who rule with iron rod and heel;
Slaves to giant combinations,
   Devoid of heart or soul to feel.
Who says ye are not slaves but lies,
   And slaves ye ever will remain,
Until like freemen ye arise
   And cast from you the tyrant's chain.

See your children starving round you,
   See your wives' pale, haggard face,
While the chains with which they've bound you,
   Keep music to your saddened pace.
Where's the soul's high aspiration,
   That ought to fill each freeman's breast?
Where's the pride of birth and nation,
   That with all freemen ought to rest?

Where's the manly independence,
   That all true freemen ought to feel?
Where's the look of bright resplendence,
   That eyes of freemen should reveal?
Where are these, ye sons of betters,
   Are ye so blind ye cannot see?
Hear the clanking of your fetters,
   And boast no more of being free.

Struggling millions toil and labor,
   Through winter cold and summer heat,
While their wealthy, grasping neighbor,
   Tramples them beneath his feet.
While coarse and scanty is their fare,
   Rich the joints their masters carve;
But while they dine on viands rare,
   For one that feasts a thousad starve.

Bound ye are in galling traces,
   And still ye boast of being free;
Go, ye cowards, hide your faces,
   Your freedom is but mockery.
Subjects for the world's derision,
   Beneath your burdens bend and groan;
Bow your heads in low submission,
   Ye dare not call your souls your own.

Stronger are the chains around you,
   Than ever forged from brass or steel;
More rentless hands have bound you,
   Than ever slave has had to feel.
Crouch ye slaves, ye abject toilers,
   And tremble neath the tyrant's rod;
Those who are your base despoilers,
   Respect not man and fear not God.

Iron chains in time may sever,
   And links of steel be rent apart;
Mortgage bonds hold fast for ever,
   Still gnawing at the victim's heart.
Like victim struggling, but in vain,
   In anaconda's fatal coil,
So ye are writhing in the chain,
   A prey to av'rice, greed, and spoil.

The knife of Shylock's at your throat,
   Nor will he any mercy show,
Redeem, when due, usurious note,
   Or out of house and home you go.
In vain to plead for mercy's sake,
   His pound of flesh he still demands;
And though your very heart may break,
   He'll turn you out from house and lands.

Must you leave the dear old homestead?
 Indeed you must, and quickly too,
And all your wishes to be dead,
 Will bring no aid or help to you.
The home where dear old mother died,
 And where your childhood days were passed;
The home to which you took your bride,
 You must relinquish at the last.

Leave you must and leave forever,
 To make room for the stranger's face;
Soon the ties will all be severed,
 That clustered round the dear old place.
In vain you plead in mournful tone,
 And ask the tyrant to forbear,
As well appeal to block of stone,
 As to the heartless millionaire.

Never mind your children crying,
 Their sobs and tears will not prevail,
All their weeping and their sighing,
 To bring relief will only fail.
The poor-house lies not far away,
 There you may go and take your brood,
Its inmates are not asked to pay
 For what they get in shape of food.

O Freedom, 'neath thy sacred name,
 What ills the people must endure;
What wrongs and insults, taunts and shame,
 Are heaped upon the suff'ring poor.
The lash that scourged old Egypt's slaves,
 Fell not upon them so severe,
As that applied by monied knaves,
 To crush the toiling masses here.

Dare ye, as freemen, raise your head,
  And 'gainst foul tyranny protest?
Has all your pride of manhood fled,
  And honor died within your breast?
Are ye of ev'ry right bereft,
  Which ye, as freemen, ought to claim?
The only one that now seems left,
  Is that to die and end your shame.

Can cowards boast of being free.
  Whose necks are 'neath the tyrant's heel?
The only freedom left to thee
  Is that to starve, or beg, or steal;
Ye're free to suffer, groan and fret
  Beneath the burdens ye must bear;
Free to labor, toil, and sweat
  To feed and fat the millionaire.

Crouch ye slaves and meanly cower;
  Before your masters kneel and crawl;
Be thankful to the money pow'r,
  That ye're allowed to live at all.
What are ye but scum and vermin,
  Whose souls unworthy are to save?
While your masters robed in ermine,
  May kick and cuff the coward slave.

Rise, ye slaves, and rend asunder
  Your fetters and the galling chain,
Break the yoke that holds you under,
  And stand as freemen once again.
March fearlessly in bold phalanx,
  And loose the grip that's on your throats,
Move forward with unbroken ranks,
  And crush the tyrants by your votes.

Let corporations know and feel
  That you're determined to be free,
And that beneath their tyrant heel,
  Base slaves no longer ye shall be.
Better die in bold endeavor
  And sleep in hallowed, honored graves,
Than in bondage live forever,
  And die at last a race of slaves.

Rouse ye, then, your fetters sever,
  Be bold to dare and brave to do,
Strike for freedom now or never,
  And cast the servile chains from you.
Fearless be and unaffrighted,
  And prove yourselves that ye are men;
Strike till all your wrongs are righted,
  And Freedom takes her place again.

Let Freedom's fires be rekindled,
  And brightly shine round ev'ry hearth;
By Shylock's be no longer swindled,
  Who crush and grind you to the earth.
Up and onward, wait no longer,
  Nail Freedom's banner to the mast,
Time will bind you all the stronger,
  And even hope will die at last.

Use not weapons meant for slaughter,
  And let not threats affright your souls,
Bloodlessly decide the matter,
  And do your fighting at the polls.
Take honest ballots in your hands,
  And firmly all your force unite,
Insist upon your just demands,
  And be not not cowards in the fight.

Rise and crush the combinations,
    And steadily your lines advance,
Down with tyrant corporations,
    And let the toilers have a chance;
Asunder break the servile chain,
    That tyrant hands have placed on thee,
Assert your manhood once again,
    And strike for Home and Liberty.

PROTECTION vs. FREE TRADE.

Large posters were posted all over the town,
    Announcing the coming of Cicero Brown;
In great flaming letters the fact was displayed,
    That matchless he stood in defense of Free-Trade.
A free invitation was given to all,
    To turn out and hear hear him at Kimberly's Hall,
And as to get in there was nothing to pay,
    I went there to hear what the fellow would say.

Stump-speakers I'd heard since the days of my youth,
    But Brown beat them all for perverting the truth;
Protection, he said, was a robber and thief,
    And all its defenders unworthy belief.
"'Tis a swindle," he cried, "and seeks for its prey,
    The poor honest toiler who works for his pay,
And takes from his purse what he poorly can spare,
    To add to the wealth of the rich millionaire."

He went on to say that, if tariffs were low,
  Great blessings upon us would constantly flow,
We could live on the best, drink savory wine, [dine.
  Like lords we could feast, and like princes could
There was nothing that grew, and nothing that's made,
  We could not enjoy had we only free Free-Trade;
Rich carpets from Turkey might cover our floors,
  And rugs made in Persia be laid at our doors.

Our foot-wear might come from the eaters of frogs,
  And good home-made leather could go to the dogs;
The best we might purchase from over the sea,
  If trade was unfettered and only made free.
Our cloth could be woven in foreigner's looms;
  Italian made head-stones be placed at our tombs;
Old England could send us munitions of war,
  And furs could be brought from the land of the Czar.

The Swiss might supply us with watches for use,
  And "Elgin" and "Waltham" could go to the deuce;
Our knives, forks, and scissors, and tools not a few,
  The workmen of Sheffield could make for us too.
The French could supply us with ribbons and hose,
  And England would gladly provide us with clothes;
She also could make for us needles and thread,
  And farmers at home could supply us with bread.

Then why, he went on, will you quietly sit,
  And humbly, like slaves, to Protection submit?
How long will you meekly its burdens endure,
  That fall with such weight on the lives of the poor?
Protection's the curse that is blighting the land,
  It spreads desolation on every hand,
It scourges the poor with a merciless rod,   [abroad.
  And stops them from getting cheap goods from

"Hold on my Free-Trader," said workingman Lee,
    "Please stop for a moment and listen to me;
Let us glance at the past, its lessons review,
    And learn what is best for the people to do;
No doubt you are earnest in what you proclaim,
    And think that Protection's a scandalous shame,
But people, of late, have been rapidly schooled,
    And now they are not half so easily fooled."

"Your Free-Trade, I think, in the past has been tried,
    And historical facts can't well be denied,
Though statements are made by Free-Traders forsooth,
    Which full well they know are perversions of truth.
In what you have said, you perhaps are sincere,
    And all your assertions sound well to the ear;
One thing you omitted, I do not know why,
    You told not where men could get money to buy."

"The rich could abundantly buy to be sure,
    But what, in God's name, would become of the poor?
By whom, or from where, would their wants be sup-
    If work for their hands was forever denied? [plied,
Declaim about buying as much as you please
    The products of labor from over the seas,
But answer me this:—If this plan we pursue,
    What will our mechanics and workingmen do?"

"How oft in the past has our beautiful land,   [hand?
    Been scourged with the lash in the Free-Trader's
How often has Hunger stalked in at the door,
    Where presence so hateful ne'er entered before?
What desolate ruin has often been wrought, [brought,
    By foreign made goods to our shores that were
Such suff'ring entailing as hard to endure,
    And bringing distress to the homes of the poor"

"Our mills and our fact'ries in idleness stood,
   While foreign made products poured in like a flood;
Mechanics and workmen lounged idly around,
   For work was a thing that could nowhere be found.
The farmer his products to sell would not try,
   For people he knew had no money to buy;
The hand of Industry lay palsied and dead.
   And progress and thrift from the people had fled."

"Our merchants and dealers were sent to the wall,
   And over the nation gloom hung like a pall;
The march of Progression was brought to a close,
   And Enterprise slumbered in deathly repose.
Distress, like a besom, swept over the land,
   And few 'neath their burdens were able to stand;
The rich became beggars, no debts could be paid,
   And Free-Trader's laughed at the ruin they made."

"Just here let us pause for a moment or two,
   And scenes of the past let us calmly review,
And judge from the past what the future would be,
   Should trade be declared unrestricted and free,
Our fact'ries deserted would fall to decay,
   Our mills standing idle would crumble away;
All labor for workmen would soon disappear,
   And Progress would stop in its onward career."

"Are these the conditions ye seek to enjoy?
   Then down with Protection, its blessings destroy,
Compete, if you will, with all nations of earth,
   And bring desolation to every hearth.
If this be your wish, that our fact'ries stand still;
   That fires be extinguished in furnace and mill;
That workshops be closed and distress should begin,
   Then open the gates and let Free-Trade come in."

O, Heavenly Father, if such be Thy will,
  To scourge and afflict us with every ill,
Send earthquakes and cyclones, and bolts from the sky,
  And pour on us phials of wrath from on high;
Afflict us with scurvy and festering sores,
  Torment us with vermin, send plagues to our doors,
Let itches and fevers upon us be laid,
  But keep from us, Father, the curse of Free-Trade.

A FRIENDLY DISCUSSION.

Upon a box one pleasant day,
  Two farmers sat in front of Dick's;
Discussing in a friendly way
  The markets, times, and politics;
With tangled beards, and unkempt hair,
  And patches on each breeches knee,
They talked of burdens hard to bear,
  And wondered what the end would be.

One smoked a pipe of briar wood,
  Blacken'd and charred from constant use;
A good sized quid the other chewed,
  And squirted out tobacco juice;
And while discussing earnestly,
  In rough, but honest, country style,
Their hands were busy as could be
  With jack-knives, whittling all the while.

For Yankee, one might well be ta'en,
　From his peculiar speech and nod;
The other's accent told quite plain,
　That he was from the Ancient Sod;
The name of one was Thomas Horne,
　That of the other, Dan McGrew;
Though patched their clothes, and badly worn,
　'Twas plain they knew a thing or two.

"I tell you what," said Mr. Horne,
　"And folks may say just what they please,
But since the hour that I was born,
　I never saw such times as these.
With taxes grievous to be borne,
　And int'rest fast becoming due,
And only fifteen cents for corn,
　I wonder where we're drifting to."

"I've been a farmer from my youth,
　And many ups and downs have seen,
But I confess, to speak the truth,
　Such times as these have never been.
Why it is so I can't conceive,
　Though some think that the worst is past,
But, Dan, I verily believe,
　From bad to worse we're going fast."

"That something's wrong, said Dan McGrew,
　"Fair minded men must all agree,
And what the farmer folks will do,
　Is really more than I can see,
Whatever stuff we have to sell,
　Will scarcely pay for horses' feed;
I tell you things are gone to hell,
　Or getting there at railroad speed."

"When wheat is only forty cents,
  And oats go begging at a dime,
I wonder what's to recompense
  The farmer for his toil and time.
The time has been when cattle paid,
  And steers a fair price would command,
But now there's nothing to be made,
  At raising stock or farming land."

"Why things should be so very low,
  I neither know nor yet pretend,
And for my life, why it is so
  Is more than I can comprehend.
Some say it is the syndicate,
  That keeps the price of products down,
But this I know at any rate,
  Meat sells for fifteen cents a pound."

"Now figure by the Rule of Three,
  And 'tis susceptible of proof,
With meat so high, a steer should be
  Worth more than two cents on the hoof.
And wheat we need not figure twice,
  Until we very plainly see,
That flour at its present price,
  Is double what it ought to be."

"I tell you what," continued Dan,
  "'Tis worse than slaves we are to-day,
To think that he who tills the land,
  Can't raise enough his tax to pay.
Here I'm a tiller of the soil
  With not a decent rag to wear,
And all the products of my toil,
  Must go to feed the millionaire."

Said Mr. Horne: "It seems to me,
  We're governed by a set of knaves,
And we who boast of being free,
  Are nothing but a race of slaves.
Slaves to trusts and corporations,
  That daily on the people prey,
Slaves to thievish combinations,
  That rob and steal from day to day."

"And then about election time,
  Some grasping shylock sounds the note,
And fellows come with cheek sublime,
  To tell us farmers how to vote.
You know, McGrew, we haven't hitched
  On politics, in years gone by,
And now I say, though I be switched,
  You have been nearer right than I."

"Republican I've always been,
  One of the strongest kind at that,
But things are so corrupt I ween,
  I'll turn and be a democrat."
"A democrat," said Dan aloud,
  "To that objection might be made,
Because you always have avowed,
  Protection is the life of trade."

"Confound Protection," Horne replied,
  "No greater wrong have we to bear,
Do wolves protect the sheep"? he cried,
  Or hounds the frightened, hunted hare?"
"Declare it by what name you may,
  'Tis but another word for fraud;
I do not care what others say,
  I call it only theft, By G——d."

"Ask the farmer who's protected,
  He'll answer with the price of wheat;
How do workingmen respect it?
  They say protection is a cheat.
Protective laws are only meant,
  More riches to the rich to give;
The sons of toil must be content,
  That they're allowed the chance to live."

" 'Tis tariff this and tariff that,
  Specific and *ad valorem*,
Tariff on coat, tariff on hat,
  And tariff to pay for joram;
There's tariff low and tariff high,
  Tariff on all the rags we wear;
And next we hear, no doubt they'll try,
  To place a tariff on the air."

A stander-by broke in to say,
  "Your language, sir, is rather strong,
And though emphatic in your way,
  I think you're altogether wrong.
Protection made us what we are;
  And surely, sir, you do not want,
To place our workmen on a par,
  With ill-paid foreign mendicant."

" 'Tis right you are," responded Dan,
  "And here examples you may see,
Of how protection helps the man,
  Who labors in this land so free.
Under what you call protection,
  On us the paupers' doom will fall;
This, and currency contraction
  Will drive us to the poorhouse all."

"In vain for work mechanics seek,
　And workmen idle must remain,
And yet some fellows have the cheek,
　To tell us we should not complain;
Of pauper labor they will prate,
　Who never soiled their dainty hands,
As though it helped our wretched state,
　To say they're worse in other lands."

"Come, Dan," said Horne, "time flies apace;
　These fellows yet may be impressed
That freedom still finds resting place,
　Within the Anglo-Saxon breast.
'Tis little that is left us now
　Worth fighting for, I must confess,
And here, most frankly I avow,
　That little's fast becoming less."

"O that some champion could be found,
　Who would the people's cause advance,
Untie the bands with which they're bound,
　And give the poor man half a chance;
Put down the trusts, reform the laws,
　From corporations set us free,
Defend the people's righteous cause,
　The cause of right and liberty."

THE FLEECERS FLEECED.

He strolled into the gambling room
   In careless sort of way,
And by the table placed himself
   To watch the players play;
He did not look as though he knew
   Enough about the game,
To make him undertake to risk
   A dollar on the same.

And there he sat quite unconcerned,
   As any stranger might,
And watched the game as though it was
   To him a novel sight;
He closely eyed them deal the cards,
   And marked each move they made,
And strictest notice seemed to take
   Of how each player played.

He sat astride upon his chair,
   A custom in the west,
And on his arms, across the top,
   His bearded chin did rest.
With gaze intent he watched the game
   As spider would a fly,
But what he thought or what he felt
   Was told not by his eye.

Though quietly the game progressed,
  The stakes were far from small;
Not "tens," but "hundreds" would be bet
  Before there was a "call;"
But there was something in the game
  Looked rather strange, he thought,
'Twas nearly always one of three
  Was sure to win the "pot."

He saw 'twas only now and then
  The fourth man ever won,
And this was only meant, he thought,
  To draw the victim on.
While silently the game went on
  The bets were still increased;
And soon the victim in their toils
  Was most completely fleeced.

The careless stranger sitting there
  Was next invited in,
But hesitated quite a while
  Before he would begin.
"I don't know much about the game,"
  He said, in careless way,
"But since I'm here, I'll take a hand
  To pass the time away."

He started rather cautiously,
  And felt his way with care,
And sometimes bet a "ten" or two
  Upon a single pair.
The "sharpers" thought they had a "flat"
  On whom to play their tricks,
But gen'rously would let him win
  About one hand in six.

His "twenties" and his "hundreds" went,
  But still he kept quite cool,
And never lost his head for once
  However big the "pool."
He kept right on and played his game
  Regardless of the cost,
And lose however much he might,
  His nerve he never lost.

The game went on, and higher yet
  The stakes would still be made,
And sometimes on a single hand
  A "thousand" would be laid.
The stranger once took up his cards,
  Then laying down the same,
He asked as though quite unconcerned,
  "Is this a limit game?"

"No, stranger, no," they answered him,
  "To limit's not the style,
The player must himself decide
  According to his 'pile.'"
Then higher still the betting rose,
  The "thousand" line was crossed;
And very soon a "call" revealed
  The stranger to have lost.

Not slightest tremor of the lip,
  Nor yet the faintest start,
Betrayed a shade of nervousness
  Upon the stranger's part;
He played like master skilled at fence,
  Who understood his place,
And waited for the time to come
  To give the *coup-de-grace*.

On went the game without a break,
    And higher grew the play,
But seldom did a run of luck
    Come round the stranger's way.
At length by chance, or by design,
    A winning hand he got,
And when they showed up all around
    He gathered in the "pot."

He dealt the cards, and round the board
    Each player took his hand,
And half the players called for "two,"
    And half for only "one."
"I go three hundred," said the first,
    "Twice that," said number two,
"And I will go," said number three,
    "Five hundred more than you."

The stranger paused, laid down his cards,
    And thought the matter o'er;
Then calmly said, "I'll see that bet,
    And go one thousand more."
The "tug of war" was on at last,
    The Greek a Greek had met,
And now 'twas pull, and tug, and strain,
    As each increased his bet.

'Twas now a battle to the death,
    Nervo took the place of skill,
The stranger meeting all their bets,
    And going higher still.
The "sharpers" kept the betting up,
    Until they staked their all,
And when they could no higher go
    It ended with a "call."

"King full I have," said number one;
  "A flush," the second said;
A "full hand" too, the third one had,
  With ladies' at the head.
The stranger then laid down his cards,
  And placed them in a line;
And said, "Four aces beat you all,
  And now the 'pot' is mine."

He raked the pile from off the board,
  And then the playing ceased,
But he they undertook to shear
  Was not among the fleeced.
The stranger found when closed the game,
  Ten thousand he had won;
And left the "sharpers" sitting there,
  All wond'ring how 'twas done.

ALICE McKEE.

As pure as the love of the angels on high;
  As deep as the ocean or fathomless sea;
As warm as the sun that emblazons the sky,
  Such measure of love I bear Alice McKee.

As tender as bud on a delicate flow'r,
  Or fresh opened leaf on a blossoming tree;
As sweet as the fragrance of rose scented bow'r,
  The love that I bear for sweet Alice McKee.

Without thee, my darling, I cannot exist;
   The world to my heart would a wilderness be;
My life would go down in the depths of the mist,
   For all would be dark without Alice McKee.

O treat me not coldly, nor look with disdain
   On him who stands pleading so fondly to thee;
O tell me not, darling, my love is in vain,
   But that I'm accepted by Alice McKee.

O joy of my life, and delight of my soul,
   As sunlight to flower so thou art to me;
The earth I would travel from center to pole,
   To win thy affection, fair Alice McKee.

Besides thee on earth there is nothing I prize;
   How worthless and trifling all else that I see;
The hope of my heart and the light of my eyes,
   Are all in the answer of Alice McKee.

Here, here at thy feet, I devotedly kneel;
   O speak to me, darling, and say that I'm blest;
But Alice replied, with a curl of her lip,
   "O dry up your nonsense, and give me a rest."

JACOB.

GEN. XXV–XXVI–XXVII–XXVIII–XXIX–XXX.

In ancient times, long, long ago,
  Three thousand years and more,
Dwelt Isaac, son of Abraham,
  On Canaan's happy shore.
He had a fond, devoted wife,
  Rebekah was her name,
But she was not a Canaanite,
  Of Syrian blood she came.

They lived a peaceful, happy life,
  Preferring peace to war;
And rich became in flocks and herds,
  Whilst dwelling in Gerar;
But though so blessed in worldly goods,
  Great sorrow was their share;
For twenty years had brought to them
  No sign of coming heir.

Rebekah wept that such should be;
  Her heart was filled with gloom,
And Isaac then besought the Lord
  That He would ope her womb.
And, as in answer to his prayer
  Rebekah then begins,
And calling Isaac to her aid
  Brings forth a pair of twins.

Each was in gender masculine,
    And first one of the pair,
As we are told, came forth all red
    And covered o'er with hair.
'Twas "nip and tuck" between the two,
    As scripture doth reveal;
The second pressed the first so close
    He held him by the heel.

"And the boys grew," the bible says;
    So much we should suppose;
Jacob and Esau they were named,
    As scripture doth disclose.
But here the latter we will drop,
    And let him pass from view,
As what we further have to say
    With Jacob has to do.

Good Isaac thought that Jacob had
    Attained that age in life,
When he should do as he had done,
    And find himself a wife;
He blessed him as a father should,
    And took him by the hand,
And charged him that he must not take
    A wife of Canaan's land.

"Arise, to Padan-aram go,"
    Thy mother's native place,
Thou'lt find 'mongst Laban's daughters there,
    Great beauty, worth, and grace.
To Isaac's wish he bowed assent,
    His will should be obeyed;
And off for Padan-aram starts
    In search of pretty maid.

The sun went down, but on he went
  Till darkness round him crept;
When on the ground he stretched himself
  And very soundly slept;
And while he slept he had a dream—
  Nghtmare was then unknown—
In which he saw a ladder reach
  From earth to heaven's throne.

Next day he journeyed on again,
  With courage bold and high,
Until he came to flocks and herds,
  With shepherds standing by;
He saw fair Rachel at the well,
  O sight extremely rare!
And e'en without a "By your leave,"
  He kissed her standing there.

When Rachel's father had been told
  That Isaac's son had come,
He ran and took him in his arms,
  And asked him to his home.
For Jacob was Rebekah's son;
  Laban was her brother;
And hence their offspring then would be
  Cousin to each other.

One day to Jacob, Laban said,
  "Why shouldst thou work for naught?"
Whate'er thou say'st thy wage shall be
  We'll settle on the spot.
Two daughters Uncle Laban had,
  One, Leah, fair and sweet,
But Jacob gave no kiss to her
  When first he did her meet.

But Rachel captivated him;
   In love with her he fell;
For was she not the charming maid
   He kissed beside the well.
"I will give to thee in service,
   Full sev'n years of my life,
If at the end thou'lt give to me
   Fair Rachel for my wife.

"Agreed," said Uncle Laban then,
   On that I give my hand;
"Much better give her unto thee
   Than any other man;
For thou art of my flesh and bone,
   My sister's younger son,
And dating from this very day,
   Thy service is begun."

So rapidly the time went by,
   The Good Book also says,
The seven years to Jacob seemed
   Just as so many days.
Then Jacob unto Laban said,
   "My service ends with you,
Now give me Rachel for my wife
   As you agreed to do."

But Laban was a sly old fox,
   And up to many tricks,
And thought by cunning scheme he could
   Get Jacob in a fix.
The Chinee has peculiar ways,
   But they pass out of sight,
Compared with those peculiar to
   The ancient Israelite.

Laban assembled all the men,
  And gave a mighty feast,
And as the wine would faster flow
  The mirth and fun increased;
And when the trap was all prepared,
  According to his plan,
On Jacob he performed a trick
  He did not understand.

At festal board I rather think,
  Too long had Jacob stayed,
Or he'd have tumbled to the trick
  That Uncle Laban played;
And though it was contemptible,
  It only serves to show,
How foxy was the Israelite
  In ages long ago.

At length festivities were closed,
  And Jacob went to bed,
But 'twas not Rachel he embraced,
  But Leah in her stead;
For Uncle Laban planned it well;
  The feast continued late;
And we may judge, from what occurred,
  What was poor Jacob's state.

But when, next morning, he awoke
  With Leah by his side,
He saw the trick that had been played
  To cheat him of his bride;
And going forth in wrothful mood,
  He unto Laban said:
"Wherefore didst thou put Leah, sir.
  Not Rachel in my bed?"

Then Laban, answ'ring, made reply:
　　"Keep down thy wrath, my son,
To give the younger daughter first,
　　It cannot so be done;
Fulfil thy week with Leah, then,
　　She's comely, fair, and kind,
And serve me other seven years,
　　And Rachel shall be thine."

When Leah's week had been fulfilled,
　　To Laban Jacob went:—
"But let me now have Rachel, sir,
　　And I shall be content."
There was no law 'gainst bigamy,
　　In patriarchal days,
But things have changed since Jacob's time,
　　For which let's render praise.

To drive from Jacob all distrust,
　　For trick that he had played,
Laban gave him both his daughters,
　　And gave to each a maid;
The latter play important parts,
　　As farther on we'll see,
In adding numbers to the stock
　　Of Jacob's progeny.

As man two masters cannot serve,
　　And honor 'like each name,
So neither can he have two wives
　　And love them both the same;
And so it was in Jacob's case,
　　As it had been before,
He loved fair Leah none the less,
　　But Rachel he loved more.

To offset this the Lord appeared,
  And opened Leah's womb;
While Rachel barren did remain,
  Which filled her heart with gloom.
Leah conceived and bare a son,
  And Reuben he was named;
The second that in due course came,
  Was Simeon proclaimed.

When Levi came as number Three,
  She felt supremely blest;
But when the fourth one, Judah, came,
  She was allowed to rest.
But grief had seized poor Rachel's heart,
  She'd weep, and sob, and sigh;
And in distress to Jacob cried:
  "Give children or I die."

Then Jacob in a wrothful mood,
  Into a passion flew,
And said the fault was not with him,
  He'd done all he could do.
"Am I," to Rachel then he said.
  "In God's stead to be placed,
Who hath withheld from thee the fruit
  Thou long'st so much to taste."

"O, Jacob, Jacob," Rachel cried,
  "Place Bilha on my knee,
And do thou go in unto her,
  And she shall bear for me."
Now Bilha was a comely lass,
  To Rachel she was maid,
And we can learn from Holy Writ,
  The noble part she played.

And Jacob hearkened to his wife,
    Placed Bilha on her knee—
O, Rachel, Rachel, fie, for shame!
    Where was thy modesty?
Maid Bilha brought him forth a son,
    And Rachel did rejoice,
And in her joy she cried aloud
    That God had heard her voice.

The maid conceived and bare again,
    For well she played her part;
The coming of the second son
    Brought joy to Rachel's heart.
"I have wrestled with my sister,
    And now prevailed have I,"
And Rachel gave to them the names
    Of Dan and Naphtali.

But Leah not to be outdone
    By Rachel at the game,
Became convinced her maid could do
    Much better, or the same.
If Bilha bare him children two,
    Why might not Zilpah three?
That she's as good as Rachel's maid,
    I'll give my guarantee.

Her estimate of Zilpah's pow'r,
    Was just a little high;
For Bilha she could not outrun
    However hard she'd try;
For Rachel's maid had set the pace,
    Leah's couldn't pass her,
And Zilpah had to quit with two:—
    They were Gad and Asher.

'Twas in the days of harvest time,
  When Reuben, prowling round
Among the fields, on Laban's farm,
  A lot of mandrakes found;
He gathered them and took them home,
  And found his mother there,
And going up to where she sat,
  He gave them to her care.

Then Rachel to her sister said:
  "I pray thee give me some:"
But Leah's jealousy was not
  So eas'ly overcome;
She answered her reproachfully,
  Reminding her of facts,
And calling her attention to
  Her underhanded acts.

"Is it to thee a matter small,"
  Said Leah, with some spite,
"That Jacob thou'lt not let me have,
  For e'en a single night,
And wouldst thou take away from me,
  The mandrakes of my son?
But let me tell you here and now,
  You shan't have even one."

"O Sister Leah," Rachel said,
  "Don't be so hard of heart;
I think of all that you have got
  You might give me a part."
But Leah stood immovable,
  Not one would she bestow;
And in the most emphatic terms,
  She told her sister so.

But Rachel had a card to play,
  That she was holding back;
As skilful player in a game,
  Who slips one from the pack.
"You say your husband I have ta'en
  Is he not mine by right?
But if the mandrakes thou'lt divide,
  He'll lie with thee to-night."

No magic wand in wizzard's hand,
  Could greater change have wrought,
And Rachel there and then received
  The mandrakes that she sought.
Then forthwith Leah to the field,
  Enraptured with delight,
And notice served on Jacob there
  To lie with her that night.

"I have hired thee," said Leah,
  "With mandrakes of my son;
And don't forget to come to me,
  When thy day's work is done."
He did as she requested him,
  And lay in her embrace,
And Issachar, in course of time,
  Was added to the race.

Once more she got him to her bed,
  And she conceived again;
But whether Rachel gave consent,
  Is not so very plain.
Between the ladies and the maids,
  Old Jacob prospered well;
To follow his example now,
  Would raise up merry hell.

The sixth time Leah was accouched,
  She really wept for joy,
To think that she had borne again
  Another bouncing boy;
"Now will my husband dwell with me,"
  'Twas thus her language run,
And to her youngest son she gave
  The name of Zebulun.

Poor Rachel was disconsolate,
  And shed most bitter tears;
And lived in utter wretchedness,
  For lo, these many years;
She felt as though her wretched life
  Had undergone a curse;
And ev'ry son that Leah had
  Made her so much the worse.

But after many weary years
  Of wretchedness and grief,
To her surprise, a change took place
  That brought her great relief;
Her yearning soul was filled with hope,
  Her grief was turned to joy;
For angel came her heart to cheer,
  In shape of lovely boy.

The bliss of motherhood was her's,
  Her cup of joy ran o'er;
"The Lord," said she, "hath ta'en from me
  The great reproach I bore;
And since **my** wailing cry He heard,
  And comfort I have found,
My darling's name shall Joseph be,"
  And thus 'twas written down.

How long' twas after this event,
  To say I won't begin,
But she another blessing found,
  In shape of Benjamin;
And thus we have the pedigree,
  As told by ancient scribes,
And as revealed by Holy Writ,
  Of Israels's dozen tribes.

One day to Laban Jacob said:—
  "Give me my wives I pray,
For whom I served you faithfully,
  That I may go away."
For Jacob never quite forgot,
  Although he little said,
How Laban had, by cunning trick,
  Put Leah in his bed.

"This haste, my son;" good Laban said,
  "I cannot understand;
Why not here tarry with thy wives,
  In this delightful land?
Thy wages but to me appoint,
  And thee I'll satisfy;
No fair demand that thou shalt make,
  Shall I to thee deny."

Said Jacob, in a surly mood,
  "I come with no demands,
And nothing thou canst give to me
  Of houses or of lands.
But there's one thing if thou wilt do,
  I then shall ask no more,
And I shall keep and feed thy flocks
  As I have done before."

"What is the thing thou'dst ask of me?"
  Make known thy wish, my son;
All that a kinsman well might do,
  For thee it shall be done."
The game of fence is now commenced
  'Tween Israelite and Jew;
Each striving by his cunningness
  The other to outdo.

Then Jacob unto Laban said:—
  "Thy flocks I shall pass through,
And all the speckled goats remove,
  And spotted cattle too;
And all the brown among the sheep,
  I also shall retire;
And when the work is all complete,
  Of such shall be my hire."

"And herewith be it understood,
  When settlement we make,
That all brown sheep and speckled goats,
  For my share I shall take;
But all the rest among the flock,
  That may not spotted be,
Including cattle, goats and sheep,
  Shall all belong to thee."

Good Laban laughed within his sleeve,
  And chuckled with delight;
For speckled lambs and kids, he thought,
  Could not have parents white;
Then taking Jacob by the hand,
  He squeezed it rather hard
And said: "My son, it shall be done
  According to thy word."

The ringstreaked and the speckled goats,
  The females and the males,
And all that had a spot of white
  On either heads or tails;
And all the brown among the sheep
  Were taken from the stock;
And three days' journey placed between
  The separated flock.

But Laban very shortly found,
  And found to his dismay,
That Jacob understood a game
  His Uncle couldn't play;
And as the light upon him dawned,
  Reproachfully he said:—
"O, woe is me, that e'er I placed
  Fair Le. in Jacob's bed."

Where Jacob got his knowledge from,
  Is not for me to say,
But sure he was a scientist
  In his peculiar way;
And who would think of such a thing,
  But son of Abraham,
That whitled sticks would make a ewe
  Bring forth a speckled lamb.

While Jacob slept, there came a voice
  From angel standing by,
And waking up, he rubbed his eyes,
  And answered: "Here am I,"
And looking up from where he lay.
  He saw to his delight,
Not "witch and warlock in a dance,"
  But much more pleasant sight.

He saw the rams the cattle leap,
   To him a pleasant view;
Not only ringstreaked did he see,
   But specked and spotted too.
But modesty will not permit
   I write another line;
The story's told in Genesis,
   'Bout chapter twenty-nine.

O, how can mortal pin his faith,
   On such a book as this?
And which in courts is still held up,
   For spotless lips to kiss;
And how can thinking men believe,
   In stories so absurd?
Yet preachers say that all the stuff
   Is God's inspired Word.

LOT.

Ev'ning shades were fast descending
　　On Mamre's plain below,
Where Sodom and Gomorrah stood
　　Five thousand years ago.
The people revelled in their sin
　　Unmindful of their fate,
When unto Lot two angels came
　　As he sat by the gate.

He did not know from whence they came,
　　From village or from camp,
But what appeared as angels then
　　Would now appear as "tramp."
Lot being of a kindly turn,
　　He friendly did them greet,
And invitation gave to them
　　To enter in and eat.

"My lords," said he, "I pray ye now,
　　The day is almost closed,
Here thou may'st tarry for the night
　　If thou art so disposed."
"Nay, nay," they said, "we'll take the street,
　　For such is our intent;"
But Lot pressed them so earnestly,
　　They yielded their consent.

No sooner were they entered in
  And furnished with a seat,
Than each with water was supplied
  With which to wash his feet;
For in those ancient, good old times,
  So many years agone,
The kid-skin shoe and calf-skin boot
  Were totally unknown.

Feet washed and dried, they gathered round
  And all together sat,
While Lot and his two stranger guests
  Engaged in friendly chat;
But soon the good wife made it known
  The table all was spread,
Then to the board they all repaired
  And ate unleavened bread.

That they a good night's rest might have,
  Clean beds had been prepared;
But ere the strangers had lain down
  Tumultuous noise was heard;
For many wicked Sodomites
  From quarters near and far,
Stood shouting just outside the house
  Like demons bent on war.

Both old and young assembled there,
  Raised fierce and angry shout.
And soon they had the house of Lot,
  Encompassed round about;
And there they stood, a howling mob,
  Like wild beasts after prey,
Demanding that the strangers should
  Come forth without delay.

The duty of a noble host
   Lot fully understood,
And going forth himself, alone,
   Addressed the multitude.
" I pray you, brethren," he began,
   "Don't do so wickedly,
Respect the strangers in my house,
   If thou hast none for me."

"Behold, I have two daughters fair,"
   For thus his speech it ran,
"Two virgins still in purity,
   As yet unknown to man;
These to your hands will I resign,
   To use as ye deem best;
But stranger guests, within my house,
   Don't injure or molest."

'Twas right that Lot his daughters should
   Believe them pure and chaste;
And that no sinful Sodomite
   Had ever them embraced;
But to dispute this point with him,
   I will not take the pains;
But, from their action in the cave,
   Some room for doubt remains.

No sooner had he thus proclaimed,
   Than forthwith came reply,
"Stand back, stand back," the rabble cried,
   "Thy offer we deny;
Why should we to this *fellow* yield,
   Who prates of chastity?
He came a stranger to our midst
   And now a judge would be."

They threatened Lot with vengeance dire,
 And pressed him very sore;
And in their rage came very near
 To breaking down the door;
But just as they were pressing on,
 And Lot's life was at stake,
The strangers sheltered 'neath his roof,
 Did not their host forsake.

The raging, shouting Sodomites
 Kept up a fearful din,
But when Lot's doom was almost sealed,
 Came succor from within;
The howling mob was pressing on
 With hate intensified,
When suddenly the door was ope'd
 And Lot was pulled inside.

With blindness those about the door
 Were smitten one and all;
And those who thus had lost their sight,
 Embraced both great and small.
But here the story is at fault,
 It does not tell enough,
And fails to say if what was used,
 Was pepper, flour, or snuff.

Lot safe, the strangers asked of him,
 "Who hast thou here beside,
Daughters, sons, or sons-in-law,
 That doth with thee abide?
It matters not where'er they are,
 Or whomsoe'er they be,
Go gather them with greatest haste,
 And from this city flee."

"For we this city shall destroy,
   Such is our mission here,
And hence it was we came to thee
   To warn thee danger's near."
When this announcement had been made,
   Lot instantly arose,
And off to warn the absent ones
   Immediately he goes.

"Up, up," he cried, "there's danger near,
   Speed forth without delay,
For Sodom's doomed to be destroyed;
   Haste, haste and get away."
But those to whom the warning came,
   With him did not agree,
And thought from his excited state,
   Demented he must be.

Next morn the angels came to Lot,
   To speed him on his way,
And urged him to depart at once
   Without the least delay;
But Lot, in hesitating mood,
   Stood lingering in doubt,
And then the angels took his hand
   And gently led him out.

"Flee, flee," the angels said to him,
   "Escape, now, with thy life,
The Lord in mercy deals with thee,
   Thy daughters, and thy wife;
Look not behind thee on the way;
   From turning back refrain;
But haste thee forth with all thy speed,
   Nor stop in all the plain."

"To yonder distant mountain flee,
　This city now is doomed,
Nor do thou linger on the way
　Lest thou should'st be consumed."
Lot was not like the Sodomites,
　A people steeped in lust,
But always lived in fear of God
　And on him placed his trust.

But still he did not like the plan
　The angel had disclosed;
And then like lawyer at the bar,
　Objection interposed.
"Not so, my Lord, not so, my Lord,"
　He earnestly did cry,
"Not to the mountain send me off,
　Lest I, perchance, should die."

"Behold, there is a city near,
　A small one, as we see,
If I've found favor in Thy sight,
　Be merciful to me;
Please change the order of the march,
　And thither let me go,
And thus unto thy servant, Lord,
　Thy greater mercy show."

The angel, answering, said to Lot,
　"In this thou hast been heard,
And unto thee it shall be done
　According to thy word;
But haste thee now to make escape
　At once thy way pursue,
For until thou art safely gone
　There's naught that I can do."

Then tow'rd the city Lot sped on
   As if for very life;
And with him went across the plain
   His daughters and his wife.
But woman, bless her angel heart,
   Will sometimes have her way,
Nor will she do, when in the mood,
   As men or angels say.

And it would seem, that long ago
   They acted just the same,
For mother Lot, the story says,
   Was disobedient dame;
She dropped a little to the rear,
   Then made a sudden halt,
And looking round, she then and there
   Became a lump of salt.

What afterwards became of her,
   The good Book doesn't say;
But, doubtless, 'neath the sun and rain
   She melted all away.
This ought a lesson to have been
   To women evermore,
But there are some perverse to-day,
   As in the days of yore.

Were all the women turned to salt,
   Who don't their lords obey,
How many husbands would be left
   To pine their lives away;
So we should all most thankful be,
   That such is not the case,
For if it were, how soon would come
   The end of human race.

And men have not improved so much
   As many of them claim,
And while they curse the Sodomites,
   They do about the same;
They practice just the same old tricks,
   Same pleasures seek to find;
But they are kept by law's restraint,
   A little more in line.

So let us all, both great and small,
   Of ev'ry rank and name,
Still bear in mind that all mankind
   Are just about the same;
Against temptation some are strong,
   And others weak and faint;
But oft the one that slips and falls,
   Is much the more like saint.

But Lot, as though quite unconcerned,
   Kept fleeing for his life,
And never turned around to see
   What happened to his wife;
At least this much we must infer,
   For in the Book we find,
That all had been enjoined alike
   To never look behind.

The sun had risen on the earth,
   When Lot arrived at Zoar,
And for his disobedient wife,
   He never saw her more;
But how they ever came to know
   That she had turned about,
Is rather catachrestical
   And subject to some doubt.

And then he looked across the plain,
   His journey at an end,
And on the fated cities saw
   Brimstone in show'rs descend;
And while in wonder there he gazed,
   Astonished at the same,
From where Gomorr' and Sodom stood,
   There rose a mighty flame.

Lot, fearing now to dwell in Zoar,
   Concluded he would go
And find some other place to dwell,
   And leave the plain below;
Then with his daughters forth he went—
   Their names are not made known—
And dwelt with them in mountain cave
   Secluded and alone.

How long they had been in the cave,
   The good Book states it not,
When both the daughters there began
   To hatch a little plot;
For feelings strange came over them,
   Which they could not explain;
They longed for something to enjoy,
   Which they could not obtain.

Said the firstborn to the younger,
   "Our father's getting old,
And not a man of all the earth
   Do ever we behold;
No man can come in unto us,
   To play with us in mirth,
Like as in other places is
   The manner of the earth.

A question here presents itself:
   How did they come to know,
About the manner of the men
   For whom they hungered so?
For Lot had told the multitude,
   "To men they were unknown,"
Yet in the cave their yearning hearts,
   Cry out for man alone.

"Now listen," said the elder one,
   "I'll tell what let us do,
And we can work a little scheme
   Right here between us two;
We'll make our father drunk with wine,
   Till all his senses swim,
Then you and I can take our turn,
   And go and lie with him."

To this the younger did agree,
   And so the plan was laid,
Which makes me doubt the truth of what
   Good father Lot had said.
But that he thought them to be chaste,
   I have no doubt is true;
But virgin maid would never act
   As they proposed to do.

The story then goes on to tell
   How well they did succeed;
And got the old man reeling drunk
   As both of them agreed;
And when in this besotted state,
   He to his bed had hied,
The elder daughter watched her chance,
   And lay down by his side.

When on the morn the daughters met,
  O, shameful to be told!
The elder to the younger said,
  "Now, hearken and behold;
With father yesternight I lay,
  We'll make him drunk once more;
And you can lie with him to-night
  And thus our seed restore."

That night when he was drunk again,
  The ancient writers claim,
Just as the elder one had done,
  The younger did the same;
But, strange to say, the old man Lot,
  So doth the story run,
No knowledge had, nor did perceive
  What he and they had done.

But when such tricks are carried on,
  They can't be long concealed;
And what was done within the cave
  Was very soon revealed;
For evidence soon came to light,
  Which proved the awful fact,
The daughters soon would mothers be,
  By their most sinful act.

In course of time Moab was born,
  The elder's son was he;
From him came forth all Moabites,
  Past, present, or to be;
The younger gave unto her son
  The name of Ben-ammi,
From whom came forth the Ammonites,
  With their posterity.

The story here comes to a close, ·
  And having reached the end,
How Lot in Sodom was not left,
  I cannot comprehend;
Nor can I see how men of sense,
  Possessed with mental light,
Can claim and say they do believe
  That God such stuff did write.

SAUL.

Said Samuel unto Saul one day,
    "Pray hearken to my word,
And unto thee I will make known
    What saith to me the Lord;
I, coming as his messenger,
    To thee glad tidings bring;
For I am sent to thee this day
    To make thee Israel's King."

"To me thus saith the Lord of hosts:"—
    'I still remember well,
When Israel out from Egypt came,
    In Canaan's land to dwell,
How Am'lek laid in wait for them,
    As they were passing through,
And smote the feeble, faint and weak,
    And many of them slew.' "

"Now, therefore, saith the Lord of hosts,
    Command that Saul prepare,
To go and slay the Am'lekites
    Nor any of them spare;
Slay male and female, old and young,
    The suckling at the breast;
The infant in the mother's arms,
    Must perish with the rest."

I don't believe the Lord of hosts
  Said any such a thing;
Or that such message e'er he sent
  To Israel's new made King;
But as the prophet of the Lord,
  The records did explore,
He found the charge that Moses gave
  Four hundred years before.

MOSES. B. C. 1451.

*"Therefore it shall be, when the Lord thy God
hath given thee rest from all thine enemies round
about, in the land which the Lord thy God giveth thee
for an inheritance to possess it, that thou shalt blot out
the remembrance of Amalek from under heaven; thou
shalt not forget it."* DEUT. xv—19.

I wonder why the prophet sought
  To charge it to the Lord;
When well he knew the Lord of hosts
  Had spoken no such word.
But in those ancient days, as now,
  The Lord had much to bear,
And people always charged him with
  Much more than was his share.

Saul took the prophet at his word,
  Nor questioned he the same,
And ordered that the people should
  All gather at Telaim; .
Two hundred thousand men of war,
  Assembled Saul before;
And Judah sent, to swell the list,
  A good ten thousand more.

Then with this mighty warlike host
  Of ancient Israelites,
He marches forth to battle give
  To all the Am'lekites;
As wheat before the reaper falls
  The Am'lekites went down;
Nor could they any safety find
  In all the country round.

Both male and female, old and young,
  Alike were slaughtered there;
The suckling babe at mother's breast,
  Not even did they spare;
Fathers, mothers, sisters, brothers,
  All perished by the sword;
While infants by the score were slain,
  And all to please the Lord.

Nor age nor sex could mercy find,
  The slaughter must proceed;
No hand was raised to aid the weak,
  No voice to intercede;
Had not the Lord commanded Saul,
  The Am'lekites to slay;
And when the order came from Him,
  Who dare to disobey?

The Am'lekites were all destroyed;
  But one alone was spared;
Agag, their King, a respite had,
  But soon their fate he shared;
Their sheep, their oxen and their lambs,
  All perished with the rest,
Except a few that Saul had saved,
  From 'mong the very best.

SAUL.

Then unto Samuel came again
   The saying of the Lord;
At least it has been written so
   In God's most Holy Word;
"That I have set up Saul for King,
   Sincerely I repent;
And much regret to such an act
   I ever gave consent."

Next morning early Samuel rose
   To go and visit Saul;
But he was told the king had gone
   To quarter at Gilgal;
When this was told, in greatest haste
   He thither did proceed,
For he was very much enraged
   At what he heard, indeed.

A kindly greeting Sam. received,
   And very well might he,
For had he not annointed Saul,
   The people's king to be?
"Now be thou blessed of the Lord,"
   'Twas thus that Saul began,
"I have, according to thy word,
   Performed the Lord's command."

But Sam. replied: "What meanest then
   The bleating that I hear,
And the sound of lowing oxen
   That falls upon my ear?"
If he had taken time to think,
   He might have understood,
The bleating and the lowing meant
   The cattle wanted food.

To answer Sam., thus Saul began
  His conduct to explain:
"These from the Am'lekites we took,
  But all the rest were slain;
A few from 'mong the best were saved,
  To offer to the Lord;
Excepting these, all they possessed
  Were slaughtered with the sword."

"And what dost think," then Samuel asked,
  "The Lord hath said to me,
No later than this very night,
  And all concerning thee;
When thou wast little in thy sight,
  Scarce known where thou didst dwell:
Did not the Lord annoint thee king,
  To rule o'er Israel?"

"And wast thou not on mission sent,
  By His direct command,
And told the service that the Lord
  Required at thy hand?
Wast thou not told in language plain,
  That Amalek was doomed;
And thou shouldst fight the Am'lekites
  Till all should be consumed?"

"Why didst then dare disobey
  The order that you heard,
When thou wert told explicitly
  That nothing shou'd be spared;
Why didst thou fly upon the spoil,
  And do this evil thing?
Thou whom I didst with oil annoint
  To reign the people's King?"

Then Saul addressing Samuel said:—
  "The Lord I did obey;
And what he ordered me to do
  I did without delay;
I slaughtered all the Am'lekites,
  Except Agag alone;
Not e'en to nursling at the breast
  Was any mercy shown."

"Of all the flocks and herds they had,
  The sheep and oxen too,
All, all were slaughtered by the sword,
  Except a very few;
And these to Gilgal have been brought
  As off'rings to the Lord,
And hence the noise of bleating sheep,
  And oxen that you heard."

Then Samuel said:—"Bring Agag here,
  The sinful Am'lekite,
Who shouldst have perished with the rest;
  But whom thou didst not smite."
Forthwith the order was obeyed,
  Then Am'lek's King was sought,
And when he was securely bound
  To Samuel he was brought.

Said Samuel to the captive King,
  In loud and angry tone,
"Thy peop'e all have slaughtered been,
  Except thyself alone;
But this was not the Lord's command,
  As given from on High;
The order was that *none* should live,
  And therefore thou must die."

Then Samuel on Agag began
     To cut and hew and hack;
And thus the prophet put to death
     The King of Amalek.
And thus through all the Holy Book,
     Like stories run their course;
A few may not be quite so bad,
     But many, ten times worse.

HOPE BEYOND THE GRAVE.

Hope beyond the grave?   Why not?
What is the grave but the feasting hall of
Worms! where these crawling slimy creatures play
Hide and seek in the darkened chambers of
Sightless eyes, and fatten on our putrid
Flesh.

Is such a dismal, gloomy, horror
Creating place as this, to be the end
Of all hope for the immortal soul?   No.
There is something innate in man which speaks
To him of a still higher and grander
Destiny.

Heed not the vaporings of
Bigots and tyrants who say there is no
Hope beyond the grave, and who would consign
The soul to their eternal and self-made
Hell; and would give over the domain of
Thought as a sporting ground to hordes of fiends
And demons.

Death they paint as a monster
Of horrible visage; instead of a
Gentle, silent messenger that enshrouds

All earthly sorrow in everlasting
Sleep.

Who say there is no hope beyond the
Grave, know nothing of the boundlessness of
God's love; and measure His greatness by their
Own littleness. No hope beyond the grave !
Horrible ! What then? Is death the great end
All? Are we, fashioned and formed in such a
Wonderful manner, and impressed with the
Image of the Great Being who brought us
Into existence, to have the gates of
Hope forever barred against us, and be
Shut out for all eternity from the
Presence of an all-wise and all-loving
Father?

Unless we are washed and cleansed in
The atoning blood, saith the preacher, we
Are forever lost; for beyond the grave
There is no hope. Where is this cleansing blood
To be found? On Calvary. Is it a
Large river or deep sea? Neither; it is
The blood of Christ, shed on the Cross nearly
Two thousand years ago. What? Do you mean
To say, that from the body of one man
Flowed blood sufficient to wash the entire
Human race through all time? Yes, all must be
Washed in the blood of Christ to be saved. How
Can we wash in that we don't see, never
Have seen, and never can see?

It is not
Meant that you should plunge into it as though
You might into a stream of water, but

That you believe that the blood of Christ is
The only means unto salvation.

It

Is in believing, then, and not in the
Washing, whereby men are saved; and unless
We believe that Spirit father and Flesh
Mother united and came together,
The result of which was a human child;
And that this child came into the world for
No other purpose than to die for the
Sins of the world; and that the shedding of
His blood was necessary to save the
Souls of sinful men; then are we cut off
From all hope beyond the grave.

Is not the
Soul of man part of the great Spirit from
Whom it came, and will it not co-exist
With it? Can anything be perfect with
One of its parts missing? The soul, being
Immortal, must exist forever, and
Be co-existent with God. Not the god
Created by man; so horrible in
Form, and so repulsive in visage, that
Soul immortal recoils horrified from
Such ungainly sight; and the essence of
Whose being is vengeance, cruelty and
Hate, untempered by either pity, love,
Or mercy. Such is the man-made god, set
Up by priests and bigots for worship and
Adoration.

The immortal soul, freed
From the environments of superstition

And fear, by which it has been held in
Bondage and darkness for centuries, could
·Not, and would not, believe that such monster
As these soul predestinators call God,
Is the author of all Beauty, Love, and
Light; all Harmony, Intelligence, and
Order.

Open your eyes that ye may see,
And your ears that ye may hear, and hearken
To the voice of Nature, and softly and
Sweetly as the rippling waters over
The shining sand, she will speak to thee of
A God who is all Light, Love, and Joy, and
Worthy of all praise and adoration.
Not vindictive, but merciful; not a
God of hate, but of love; not cruel, but
Tender, kind, and compassionate, ever
In sympathy with the creatures of His
Creation.   One who succors in distress,
Soothes in sorrow, comforts in affliction,
And who has a healing balm for ev'ry
Wounded heart.

As mother love goes out to
Her children, and her heart yearns for those who
Are not; so God's boundless love goes out to
His children, and His great loving arms are
Ever ready to receive them.   The untold
Millions of the human race, embracing
All kindreds, tribes and tongues, all sprang from the
Same eternal source—God.   All are children
Of the same Fatherhood.   King, potentate,
Priest, prince, and beggar, are joint heirs to, and

Partakers of His immeasurable
Love.   When the caskets in which our souls are
Encased shall be laid away in the cold,
Dark grave, to become the play-house of worms;
The immortal part of our being, the
Soul, shall spring far beyond the boundaries
Of the dark and narrow cell, and take its
Flight to the presence of Him, by and through
Whom it came into existence.

Spirit

Life is eternal.   Hope survives death.   When
We have crossed the river of Time, and have
Cast off the earthly cerements by which
We are bound, then shall the soul, like glorious
Orb of day shooting from beneath the cloud,
Or caged eagle set at liberty and
Rising toward the sun—soar into the great
Beyond, to dwell forever with Him from
Whom it came.

The abyss of death can not
Stay the upward flight of Hope.   It does not
Terminate in the tomb.   The grave may be
Dark, but there is light beyond.   When we have
Left the "valley of the shadow" behind,
And have passed through the portals that lead to
The realms of the mysterious Unknown,
God's love will be there.   He does not deal with
Children after the manner of men.   His
Love never changes; the same yesterday,
To-day, and forever.

To him who reads
The book of Nature, and opens his heart

To the lessons it teaches, it is past
Understanding how the Author of so
Much that is beautiful, and proclaims so
Eloquently of love, can be such a
Monster as preachers paint him.   The birds of
The air sing of His love; the flower-clad
Fields and smiling valleys proclaim His great
Loveliness; the beasts of the forest make
Known His goodness, and even the insects
Chirrup forth His praise.   Of all His creatures,
Man alone has attributed to Him
Such hideous visage and repulsive
Form, that the soul becomes horrified at
Even the contemplation of monster
So grotesque.

        Man-made god is of stern and
Forbidding features; but Nature's God is
Of bright and shining countenance, ever
Beaming in its loveliness.   The former
Is all hate, the latter all love.   One is
Repellant, the other attractive.   One
Is vengeful, the other merciful.   One
Is cruel, the other affectionate,
Kind and loving.   The love of one is so
Small it can reach only to a few; but
So great and comprehensive is the love
Of Nature's God for his children, that it
Extends to all nations, tribes and kindreds.
Jew and Gentile, Christian and Heathen, prince
And mendicant, have all a share in the
Boundless love of Nature's God, the great and
Bountiful Being, the effluence of

Whose light divine fills all space, permeates
All matter, reaches all hearts.

                  Blessed Hope!
The shadows of the darkness of the grave
Can never fall upon thee. Over death
Thou art conqueror. Death? Separation.
Parting of the mortal and immortal.
No grave so deep, no abyss so wide, but
Hope can overleap.

                  Hope beyond the grave?
Yes. Far beyond the dark and narrow cell,
The soul will take its flight to regions of
Eternal day, and, putting on the robes
Of immortality, shall take its place
With the numberless multitude in the
Enjoyment of that hope which shall lift it
Higher and higher, until it stands in
The sight of God justified, purified,
Sanctified, glory-crowned, in the perfect
Enjoyment of the supreme bliss, joy, and
Happiness, which the great loving Father
Hath reserved for all His children.

www.ingramcontent.com/pod-product-compliance
Lightning Source LLC
Chambersburg PA
CBHW060531030726
47498CB00004B/1156